Neverpeak Mountain
Magestic Mountain
Mermaid Lagoon
Pirate Island
Maze of Regret
Tiki Forest
Neverland
Neverbay

Skull Rock
Cannibal Cove
Lost Boys Hideout
Pixie Hollow
Crocodile Creek
Pirate's Cove
Indian Tribe

PAN

TALES FROM NEVERLAND

PAN

TALES FROM NEVERLAND

DARK FAIRY TALES
BOOK 2

S. CINDERS

Dark Fairy Tales Series

PRINTED IN THE UNITED STATES OF AMERICA

"I suppose it's like the ticking crocodile, isn't it? Time is chasing after all of us."
-J.M.Barrie, Peter Pan

This story is dedicated to my readers. May you escape the constricts of time, even if it's only between the pages of a book.
My love to you... Cinders

I remember him looking round the cover and whistling to himself as he did so, and then breaking out in that old sea-song that he sang so often afterwards:

"Fifteen men on the dead man's chest—

Yo-ho-ho, and a bottle of rum!"

-Robert Lewis Stevenson, Treasure Island

1

EBONY

"There's never a man looked me between the eyes and seen a good day a'terwards . . . "

-ROBERT LEWIS STEVENSON, TREASURE ISLAND

I sent the whip flying out and didn't flinch when it struck the sailor's back with a resounding crack.

"Where is it?" I spat.

The hardened sailor winked at me, showing his blackened teeth. "A little harder, Captain. I like it dirty!"

Sighing, I summoned my first mate, Alexander Smead.

"I want to know where Princess Tiger Lily's crown is," I said as I handed the whip over to Smead. "Do not show him any mercy. As the man said, he likes it dirty."

Smead turned to whisper in disgust, "If his dick gets any bigger, I am out. This is supposed to be torture, not cheap thrills."

I forced myself to remain calm. Good help was hard to find, and Alex had been my best friend throughout my entire life.

He was also lazy, a womanizer, crude, smart as fuck, and a whole host of other things that at present I didn't care to mention.

"I don't care what you do to him, Alex. Just find out the location of the crown."

Alex's eyes lit with glee. "Consider it done."

Turning to the prisoner, I saw he no longer held that smug look.

Good.

To Alex, I added, "I have other business to attend to. But do not worry, I have found a replacement."

"Wait!" The sailor eyed the brawny Alex. All six-feet of raw Latin masculinity with messy dark hair and a scruffy black beard. "I will talk!"

Alex laughed, his perfect white teeth in contrast to his tanned skin.

"Of course, you will. But not until we have a bit of fun first."

I walked away to the sounds of the man screaming in terror. Just another day on the high seas for me. Since my father, Captain James Bartholomew Hook retired, things had been a bit dull.

I plopped down in the captain's chair that had once belonged to him. I had sailed with my father for as long as I could remember. I have no memory of my mother. Days in the past were filled with daring escapes and epic battles with the infamous Pan. But once he left with Wendy Darling and her brothers, things seemed to grow rather tedious.

My father had only one request when he passed on the Captain Hook legacy to me, and that was to kill Pan. But how was one to do that when he had disappeared into what Wendy had called, 'the real world.'

Whatever that meant.

It had been fourteen years since his disappearance. Fourteen years ago, I had been dressed as a boy gallivanting around on my father's ship in breeches and nicking the liquor from the Galley.

At the age of nine, Pan had fascinated me to no end. I was positive that I would be the one to run him through. But my father hadn't allowed me to get anywhere near the boy. Pan, not quite a man, had never seemed terribly dangerous to me. And I wasn't afraid of him.

I just wished to hell I could find a way to go after him, and then the Princess came to me for a favor. If I found her crown, she would grant me a boon. The chase led to this moment, and I was steps away from finding out how to leave Neverland.

There was a knock on my door, and I sprang to my feet. "Come in."

Alex turned the knob, he was impossibly handsome, and a right pain in my ass.

"Oh," I flopped back down in my chair, "it's only you."

He sighed dramatically, "Most ladies swoon in my presence, Eb."

"Then take a bath! I am certain your stink could knock a grown man out."

His lips twitched. "Hateful as always."

I smiled. "Did you get the location?"

"Do the mermaids like to suck my…"

I cut him off, "Eww, Alex not the image I need to be planted in my brain!"

He laughed, "Just the same, I had Potter plot out the coordinates, and we are sailing there as we speak.

"Where is it this time?" I grumbled.

"Buried in Blind Man's Bluff," Alex shrugged. "Do you ever get the impression that we have done this all before?"

Yes.

Only about a hundred million times.

"Why do you say that?" I straightened in my chair.

"It's just that sometimes, I feel like we are sailing around in circles. Neverland isn't that big."

"We are leaving Neverland," I raised my hand to stop his question. "You cannot tell anyone, Alex. But I am finding a way out of here so that we can finally acquit my father."

"How?" he breathed. Then it was as if the light turned on. "Princess Tiger Lily!"

"I have a feeling that she will be willing to trade the fairy for her crown."

"Tinkerbell?" Alex's lips curved down. "She's a right bitch, you do know that, right?"

I winced, "I know. But we need that pixie dust in order to make the ship fly."

I walked over to my father's journals.

"It says here that the ingredients are faith, trust, and pixie dust."

A wide grin spread across Alex's face. "You are leaving out thinking a happy little thought."

I gagged. "I will have happy thoughts when I deliver Pan's head to my father."

Alex grinned. "Sounds good to me!"

It wasn't too long before we had sailed to Blind Man's Bluff. The dirt where the crown was buried hadn't even settled yet. As I glanced around there were seven or eight previous hiding places in sight. Alex was right. We had done this all before.

I grabbed the crown, and we sailed for the Indian Camp near Marooners Rock. It took less than a day, and we had sailed half the length of Neverland.

"What boon would you like, Captain?" Tiger Lily had lovely golden skin, with dark eyes, and silky black hair that hung down her back.

"I would like Tinkerbell," I responded clearly.

"You can't have a person!"

For a moment, the facade of the perfect Princess fell, and Tiger Lily gaped at me.

"I need the pixie to travel beyond our world," I explained.

Tiger Lily narrowed her eyes. "Where are you going?"

I hedged. "To explore new lands and new seas."

She shook her head. "No. Tell me the truth, Captain. You are wasting my time."

I gritted my teeth not wanting to share my voyage plans with her. But I knew that if I wasn't forthright, I could lose this boon.

"I am chasing Pan!"

The words tumbled out of me at a rapid pace, "I will avenge my father, and bring back Pan's head on a platter, to feed to the crocodiles."

"Chasing Pan?" Tiger Lily seemed to be pondering the idea. "Time runs differently in the real world. Pan could be dead. For all we know, hundreds of years have passed."

"I have considered that," I clenched my fists. "But Pan wasn't born in that world. He was born in Neverland. We stop aging at twenty-five. So, even if time has passed where he is, Pan will still be alive."

Tiger Lily's lips curved into a smile. "Chasing Pan, what a singular idea."

I didn't like the sound of that.

"I would like to see that rogue again. He did steal my first kiss after all."

"We aren't going to kiss him," I ground out. "We are going to kill him."

She pouted, "Not one kiss?"

"No!" I had to be firm.

"I will promise you the pixie on two conditions," Tiger Lily grasped my hand." Are you amenable, or will you find another way to chase your enemy?"

There was no other way, and she knew it as well as I did.

"Fine!" I ground out. "What are your conditions?"

"I come along on the voyage!"

I heard Alex moan behind me, but I ignored it.

"Done," I nodded, "What else?"

"One kiss," her eyes gleamed. "Pan gets one kiss before he dies."

One kiss that could be the kiss of a blade as it slices through the skin.

"Tiger Lily, we have a deal."

2

EBONY

"What in the hell is this, Alex?" I fumed, storming down the deck.

Alex stood there with three gorgeous men, all looking smug.

"Why are Nibs, Cubby, and Tootles here? We have no need for lost boys in this venture!"

Nibs wrinkled his aquiline nose, while Cubby folded his arms across his muscular bare chest. Didn't they own shirts?

"We don't go by Nibs, Cubby, and Tootles any longer," Tootles scowled. He pointed to Nibs and Cubby, "This is Nate and Charlie, and I am Tom. You can at least allow a man to grow up, Captain."

It had been years since I had seen them. I hardly recognized the boys—men, I suppose I should say.

"Right," I cleared my throat. "Now, get your asses off my ship!"

Alex stepped up. "Not so fast, Eb. We are going to need extra crew. Several of our men have abandoned ship. They don't want to leave Neverland."

I glowered. "Who told them we were leaving?"

Princess Tiger Lily walked up, her long dark hair swaying perfectly behind her.

"Oh," she covered her mouth innocently. "Was that a secret?"

"Yes, it bloody well was a secret," I rolled my eyes. "Look it doesn't matter, I am not taking lost boys on a trip to kill Pan. They will turn on us. It is a recipe for disaster."

Charlie raised a hand. "Now, Captain. Pan deserted us to go with Wendy. When he left, we started to grow older just like all the residents of Neverland. Now we are stuck being called 'lost boys' as grown men. I am not saying I want you to kill him. But that's between you and him. I won't interfere either way."

Nate nodded. "Same, I just want to get off this bloody island!"

Tom added, "We are hard workers. You won't find us lazing about."

My eyes flashed to Alex, who immediately straightened.

Tiger Lily stepped forward. "Let them come, Captain Hook. We all deserve one great adventure in our lives, don't we? And besides, they are quite nice to look at."

Alex frowned, while Charlie blushed profusely. Tom and Nate grinned at Tiger Lily, and I could barely contain groans of exasperation.

"This isn't a pleasure cruise. I expect you all to work."

They all nodded, expectantly.

"Did you bring the pixie?" I questioned Tiger Lily.

She walked a few paces back, and I noticed that every male eye was glued to her shapely ass.

Pleasure cruise indeed, this was turning into the damn Love Boat, not the Jolly Roger.

Tiger Lily picked up a cage that was covered by a blanket. The moment she removed the covering I was greeted by the middle finger of a very angry Tinker Bell.

"Perfect!" I smiled for the first time that morning.

The voyage began with little fanfare. My father had been ill and wasn't able to see us off. I tried not to worry about him, but it was unusual to contract an illness in Neverland.

Charlie, Nate, and Tom were true to their word. I hated to admit it, but things on the ship were running more smoothly than they had in quite some time. Tiger Lily, being the true princess that she was, didn't do a damn thing.

I hadn't expected her too, and yet it still grated on my nerves.

That wasn't the worst of it. Tiger Lily was under the impression that we were 'friends.'

"Ebony," She was lying across my berth, reading the latest copy of, 'GLAMOR vs. GLAMOUR.'

"What, Tiger Lily?" I still struggled at the social graces.

She cocked her head to the side, pouting her perfectly pink lips. "I think that you could be rather attractive, if you would only try."

I looked down at my grubby pirate gear. It had been my fathers. While it was way too large and ill-fitting, it did bring me a sense of comfort.

"When was the last time you washed your hair?" She wrinkled her nose.

I scowled. "I bathe daily, Tiger Lily!"

"Do you comb it?"

I flushed. I didn't have a mother around, and pirates never worried about what their hair looked like.

"Go to hell!" This was my standard reply whenever she pissed me off, which was often.

She smiled. "I wonder what it looks like, when it's not all matted up like that?" I found one of my hands reaching up to touch the mess that I usually tied into a ponytail. Was it that bad? I didn't look in a mirror very often, but almost involuntarily, my feet walked over to the oval mirror that was above my wash basin.

Two gray eyes stared back at me above a straight nose, high cheekbones, and a cupid's bow mouth. I also had what most would consider a rat's nest living on my head and dirt on my face from the rigging.

I looked back at her. "Not every girl is beautiful, Tiger Lily."

She narrowed her eyes. "That, Ebony, is where you are wrong."

Tiger Lily then spent the next four hours trying to detangle my hair. I cannot tell you how much coconut oil was used nor the number of curse words that spewed from my lips.

"Why do people do this to themselves?" I pouted, as she washed the oil out for what had to be the fiftieth time.

"It wouldn't be so bad if you had bothered to brush it in the last decade. There!" She turned me around and grabbed the mirror.

My wet hair was the color of fresh chestnuts. It was thick and had a bit of a curl to it. It fell just below my breasts. My face had been freshly scrubbed, and my lips had a sticky substance on them that made them shine.

"What did you do to me?" I grabbed the mirror out of her hand, staring at my reflection. I looked like a girl…no, like a woman.

Tiger Lily grinned. "This is only the beginning!"

I found my clothes being ripped from my body. She was rather strong for a Princess.

"You wrap your breasts?" she recoiled in horror.

I flushed. "They are obnoxiously large, and I can't fit into my father's shirts unless I do."

Tiger Lily huffed. "You need a corset. Thankfully I have plenty."

She raced off, and I looked down at the coarse cloth I had used to wrap my breasts. Slowly I began to unwind the fabric, wincing when the blood rushed back into my flesh.

My breasts were full for my slight frame, and I had always been embarrassed by them. I cupped them in my hands wondering what they were really necessary for anyway.

Tiger Lily walked in with an armful of clothing.

"Gracious," her eyes widened.

"What?" I said defensively.

She shook her head. "Never mind. Let's get you out of those drawers, seriously Eb, could you not wear lady's underwear?"

No one had ever given me a choice.

"I thought this was what everyone wore?"

She held up a scrap of peach lace. “And you mocked me for packing too much. It is a good thing I did.”

Little did I know that things were about to become a whole lot more intrusive.

3

EBONY

"Holy shit! That hurts!"

Tiger Lily grunted, as she pulled the strings of the bustier, "Just a bit more! There! You look amazing."

I could barely see my feet—my breasts had been pushed so far into the air.

"Are you sure this is how it is supposed to look?" I had to ask. "Your breasts don't look like they are being offered on a platter."

Tiger Lily made a face. "We all can't be as well-endowed as you are, Ebony. Trust me. If I had a set like yours, I would make sure everyone knew about it."

I laughed. "Boobs-a-million? Or perhaps Breasts-r-us?"

She giggled. "Exactly. Now, you have a choice between these two tailored jackets. They will go perfectly with the black bustier. Considering you chose those tight, plum, leather pants, I would recommend the black or the charcoal. We can mix and match so that you have enough outfits to last the trip."

"I have to wear different sets of clothes every day?" I knew I was whining, but this was brand new territory for me.

"Yes," Tiger Lily let out a tiny puff of impatience. "If you can chase down Pan you can change your underwear."

Good point.

"Fine," I agreed, "but I am not curling my hair every day, that took forever."

Long ringlets decorated my head, and I must admit that the look was arresting. However, I'd managed to burn myself eleven times in the process.

Being a lady was dangerous.

Tiger Lily conceded, "You don't have to curl your hair daily, but it has to be brushed, that is non-negotiable."

"Deal," I grinned at her. "What now?"

A knowing smile curved her lips. "Now, we show you off."

The first man on my crew to see me ran straight into a wall.

The second and third stopped eating mid-bite.

As I made my way onto the deck, I heard the murmurs of approval. But it wasn't until sweet Charlie looked up from swabbing the bridge, that I blushed.

"Fuck me," he whispered, the mop clattering to the wood below.

Nate and Tom whipped their heads around and fell on their asses in the process.

It was only Alex who gave me a good dose of reality.

"Have you done something different with your hair?" his eyes narrowed as if searching.

Tiger Lily marched right up to him and started bashing him with her tiny fists.

"You will not ruin this for her. Ebony looks beautiful, and you know it!"

"Stop!" Alex tried to deflect her blows, "I am sorry, stop!"

Tiger Lily stamped her foot. "Don't tell me you are sorry!"

Alex looked at me ruefully. "I am sorry that I teased you, Eb. I have never seen you look more lovely."

She elbowed him.

"What?" he complained, trying to move away.

"Tell her that she is gorgeous and that this is how she was meant to be. Tell her that you are proud of the lady she is becoming. For heaven's sake, you are her best friend, act like it!"

Alex looked at me, panic written across his face. "Erm, what she said."

Tiger Lily stomped on his foot, and I couldn't help the bubble of laughter that escaped my lips.

"Thank you, Alex. But more importantly, thank you, Tiger Lily. I thought that Alex was my only friend in this world. But it would appear that I was mistaken."

Tiger Lily beamed at me. "Please call me Lily, I have always wanted to be your friend."

"Me?" I said dumbly. "Why?"

She walked over and took my arm. "Ebony, you are brave and courageous. You never let anything stand in your way. I admire that about you."

I glanced over at Alex who was making a hasty retreat. "I also have a rather good-looking best friend."

Lily turned ten shades of red. "Oh? I hadn't really noticed."

I barked out a laugh. "Just like he doesn't notice the instant you walk into a room, his eyes follow you everywhere you go?"

Lily stopped, arrested. "No! Tell me, do they?"

I shook my head in amusement., "Yes, you ninny. It's like watching an awkward dance that neither partner knows they are participating in. I can't look away."

Lily began to smile, "What about you? I have noticed that Nate, Charlie, and Tom hang on your every word. And that was before you learned how to tame that hair."

We walked over to the stern, glancing at the star-studded universe around us. Tinker Bell's' pixie dust 'had certainly enabled the Jolly Roger to lift from the sea and fly out into the cosmos.

We had been sailing through the skies for days now. Surely we had to be close to where Pan was hiding.

"I am not interested in the boys that way," I motioned to the vastness around us. "There will have to be someone that can tear me away from all of this to capture my heart. And to be honest, I don't think the man exists."

Lily patted my arm. "You never know what the future holds."

"Land!"

I looked up at the crow's nest to see Tom looking through the telescope.

"Captain! There is a planet ahead, do you want us to explore it?"

I raced back to my cabin and grabbed Tink's crate.

"Alright, Tinkerbell, I need to know if this is where you found Peter."

She gave me an uninterested face.

I wished to hell that I knew what she was saying, but the words only came out as tiny little bells.

I took the cage up to the deck, "Does any of this look familiar?"

Off to the east, I could see a round, blue and green planet covered with swirling, fluffy, white clouds.

Her face said it all.

"Set your course! We are on the right path!"

The rest of the voyage was filled with hard work and freezing temperatures.

I had to agree with Alex when he stated, about space, 'it was cold enough to freeze the balls off a brass monkey.'

"Batten down the hatches, men!" I shouted, as we entered the atmosphere. This world was so much larger than Neverland. I hadn't dreamed it could be so immense.

At least at this point we were warm, terrified and most likely apt to burn up in the atmosphere—but warm.

"Tink, where is Pan?"

She shrugged her shoulders as if implying she hadn't a clue.

But we both knew that was a load of horse shit.

I shook the cage, and she glared at me.

"Ugh! I wish you were full-size!"

Tink's eyes grew round and gleeful.

Suddenly the crate burst apart in a frenzy of pixie dust. I coughed as it flooded my mouth and eyes.

"What in the hell, Tink?"

"Be careful what you wish for."

I rubbed my eyes and then did once again for good measure.

"Am I dreaming?" I blurted out.

"Do you often dream of me?" Her snarky tone fit perfectly with her personality.

"How did this happen?"

Standing before me was Tinkerbell, but she was at least five-foot-seven, a good three inches taller than I was.

Her tiny green outfit was positively indecent on a grown woman.

"You wished for it," she grinned happily.

"How long will you be this way?"

Tink paused. "I hadn't thought of that. I suppose once your wish is over. Although, if you want help finding Pan I suggest we work out a deal."

"Of course, I want to find Pan!"

Tink smiled seductively, and I turned my head to see Charlie, Nate, and Tom falling all over themselves to get a glance at the pixie turned pin-up model.

This could be a problem.

4

EBONY

Tinkerbell led us over the rooftops and across the seas. Every time we thought we might be close she changed course. I was beginning to think that she hadn't a clue as to where Pan was hiding.

To make matters even more unpleasant, she was worse than a cat in heat. It took two days of her being human-sized to have the whole ship in turmoil.

She had insisted that she hadn't wanted tan lines. But when I came out to find her stark naked swinging in a hammock, I knew something had to be done.

I assigned Charlie to be her jailer. But the next day I heard groaning and moaning from his cabin. I crashed in to save him only to find Tinkerbell's lips wrapped around his cock. This was an entirely new side to Charlie that I had hoped never to see.

I couldn't help but notice his washboard abs, and the way his face looked when she pulled off. There was a pop as his massive dick came out of her mouth with a string of saliva that still connected them.

"Do you mind?" Tink winked at me.

I stammered my excuses and quickly shut the door. But I never had encountered anything remotely like that before. Sure, I had been raised on a ship and knew all the bawdy jokes. But I had never seen it firsthand.

I stumbled into Lily who couldn't help the peals of laughter escaping her lips.

"Did you just walk in on them?" her eyes danced.

"Lily, you would not believe what I just saw! She was on her knees, and he was standing there with his hands in her hair. And his dick, holy shit! It was like a cucumber, Lily!"

She doubled over, tears appearing in her eyes. "It sounds like you got a pretty good look!"

My eyes were like saucers. "Oh, I saw it all!"

"What did you see?" Alex came down the stairs with a grin on his handsome face.

Lily blushed, but I relayed it all to him—spit included.

He turned as pink as Lily, "Fuck! Don't tell me anymore!"

I frowned. "I don't see why you should be embarrassed. You were the one who said the mermaids like to suck your…"

Alex covered my mouth. "That's enough sharing for today!"

But Lily wrinkled her nose in disgust and turned to walk away.

Alex hauled me into my cabin before he removed his hand.

"Thanks a lot, Eb! Now she thinks I am some kind of pervert!"

I laughed. "You are a pervert!"

He scowled. "I don't want her to think that!"

"I don't believe it! Little Alex has a crush!"

"Shut the hell up!" Alex slumped into a chair, "I do not have a crush!"

I sprawled in the Captain's chair. "If it makes you feel any better, I think she has a crush on you as well."

Alex bolted up; eyes hopeful. "Do you really think so?"

"Well, yeah," I snorted. "Before she found out that every fish in Neverland has had a taste of your dick!"

Alex threw himself down. "Aww, shit."

Whatever I had been about to say was cut short when Tom came pounding on my cabin door.

"Captain, we have finally found Pan's location!"

Triumph glittered in my eyes. "Well, done! Round up the crew, all hands on deck."

It was a short fifteen minutes later that we met as a crew on the deck of the Jolly Roger.

"Where are we?" someone asked.

I tried to see what was below us. It honestly looked to be a maze of metal and flashing lights.

"It's New York City," Tink said happily, rubbing her hands together. "And Pan has just entered that dance club over there to the left."

"Why do they not see us?" Nate questioned.

"They don't believe in magic," Tink waved him off with a roll of her eyes. "Unless there is a child looking up, and even then most children have given up on magical things. But say there were, the adults would never believe them and since they cannot see the ship for themselves it's a non-issue."

"What is the plan?" Alex asked me.

I pulled my dagger out. "We find him and kill him. Should be easy."

Tinkerbell's eyes grew round. "You cannot just take a weapon into a club. They will haul you away, before you ever set eyes on Pan. You have to be stealthier than that."

I could be stealthy…maybe.

"What do you suggest?" I put it on her.

"You, me and Lily will go down and check out the situation, see if we can locate Pan, then return here, to decide our next move."

It sounded logical, so I was in- until I saw what they wanted me to wear to the club- then I was out.

"I don't think this is even a skirt!" I could feel air brushing against my bare ass.

"Stop being a baby," Tink leaned over to put more gloss on her lips, and I saw everything her mama gave her. "You have on more than I do."

I frowned, "The lamp shade has on more than you do, Tink."

Lily had on some leather pants and a black bra. They told me I couldn't wear the pants because the matching leather bra wouldn't fit me. Since I was required to wear the bustier, a mini skirt was my only option.

The lace panties had gotten on my nerves, but they were nothing compared to the thong. It was like wearing floss for your ass. I tried to pull it out about a million times, before Tink yelled at me to go commando.

I teetered in the sky-high boots that they'd roped me into wearing. Someone was going to end up in tears tonight, and I prayed it wasn't me.

Tink sprinkled us with dust, and we flew over the side of the deck and down to the street below, into an alley just a block from the club. I could actually hear the beat of the music from where we were.

It was sultry and heady, nothing like the music we had in Neverland. I found myself being drawn to it. We walked up to the club, and I noticed a long line of people waiting to get inside. Flicking my hair back, I marched to the front where some large men were eying the three of us carefully.

"Are you on the list?" one of the brutes asked us.

Lily raised her head impervious, "I am Princess Tiger Lily, I do not need to be on a list. I am accepted everywhere."

"Do you know what she is talking about?" the other one asked.

The first man shrugged his shoulders, "Nah, but they are hot as hell. The boss won't mind."

They unlocked the rope and beckoned us forward. Tinkerbell was eyeing the guards like they were dinner.

I had to yank her hand to get her to follow. Inside, the club was dark and smelled of perfume and something I didn't recognize. The music was so loud that I had a hard time concentrating.

Lily and Tink were just as wide-eyed as I was. The bodies on the dance floor weren't performing any dances I knew. It seemed that they were making love with their clothes on. Not that I had a whole lot of experience there, but I had seen Charlie and Tink.

A man brushed up next to me. "Hey beautiful, do you want to dance?"

I stiffened. "No thank you, kind sir."

His lips twitched, "I will be kind to you, if you let me."

What the hell?

"Um, no thank you, as I said. Doing just fine on my own. Run along now," I did some shooing movements with my hand.

"Rocko, is everything okay?"

The deep voice had my thighs clenching. If the man who belonged to that voice wanted to dance, I would be wrapping myself around him as soon as possible.

Rocko froze. "Everything is fine, boss, just getting to know these ladies."

"I will take it from here."

My pussy throbbed just listening to him. I had to see what he looked like.

Turning away from Rocko I tried to catch a glimpse, but my heels didn't move as quickly as my body, and I started to fall.

I felt strong arms grab me. One under my knees and the other around my chest. "Woah there! It's okay, I have you."

I looked into the greenest eyes I had ever seen. His chiseled face had a few days' worth of whiskers and dark brows that slanted down in concern.

His lips were perfectly shaped, and I wondered what they tasted like. I couldn't tell the color of his hair, but I could see that it was thick and wavy. I wanted to sink my fingers into it and discover its softness.

"Are you okay?" His minty breath brushed my upturned face.

"I don't know," I answered honestly.

It was then that two things happened which I shall never forget.

Lily gasped, "Your ass is showing!"

Just as the color leached from Tink's face. "Peter Pan."

Shit.

5

EBONY

I felt the man tremble, as he held me in his arms. Gasping, I pushed out of his grasp and nearly flopped onto the floor. He held me against his chest, until I was steady.

"What did you call me?" he was glaring at Tink.

She winked saucily, "It is you! Peter, I have missed you!"

Tink leaped into his arms and tried to smother his face with kisses. All the while Lily and I were staring. How could this positively gorgeous piece of man be the infamous Peter Pan? He looked dangerous, nothing like the playful youth that I remembered from my past.

Peter pushed Tink off of him, forcefully. "I am not who you think I am."

I felt a wave of relief wash over me.

"You are Peter," Tink stated emphatically.

"We can't discuss this here," Peter looked at the other man, Rocko, "We will be in my office. Do a sweep of the bar, if you could. I was headed there."

Rocko nodded and walked away looking powerful in his black suit. But he was nothing compared to Peter.

As we followed him to his office like little lambs, I couldn't help but think that I was in way over my head. The strength of his powerful shoulders underneath his suit jacket mesmerized me.

"You can't kill him," Lily hissed. "Remember! You promised me there would be a kiss."

My face heated at the picture her words brought to mind. Rather than the kiss of my dagger at his throat, I pictured Peter's lips crashing down on mine. I had never kissed a man before and found myself curious as to what a man tasted like. More specifically, I wanted to know what he tasted like.

Peter stopped suddenly, and his eyes flew to mine. My body felt like it erupted into flames as his green eyes took in every inch of my corseted chest and tiny skirt.

He swallowed his Adam's apple bobbing as he opened the door to another room.

"Please, we can discuss things further inside."

Was it just me? Or did his voice sound huskier than before?

Peter's eyes never left me as I crossed in front of him in my wobbly heels and made my way into his office. It was sleek and modern, with all sorts of inexplicable and mysterious contraptions.

A large part of me wanted to explore. That was just my nature as a pirate, that and plunder. I had always liked plundering.

"Tink," his voice brought me back to the present. "Why, after all these years have you sought me out?"

Tink pointed at me. "Because Captain Hook wanted to kill you."

At this point, I could have killed her.

I blushed. "How do you do?

His lips twitched. "You are terribly polite for Captain Hook's emissary. I am quite well. Out of curiosity, are you here to murder me?"

A wrinkle formed between my brows. This wasn't how things went in Neverland.

"But not before I kiss you!" Lily blurted out.

Peter's eyes widened, "Princess Tiger Lily, I almost didn't recognize you."

She beamed, "I am all grown-up now."

His eyes settled back to me as he answered her, "Yes, I can see that."

I felt the place between my thighs heat.

"It's only been fourteen years, Peter," Tink smirked. "Although, your 'real world' looks much different than it did when I first found you lurking in a lady's boudoir."

Peter drew a breath. "Please sit down."

We each took a seat in the plush chairs in front of his large desk. There was a window behind us that looked out over the city, and I was captivated by the lights and bustle below.

Peter settled into his large desk chair. "It might have been fourteen years for you, but it's been well over a hundred for me. Forgive me, but those times seem more like a dream."

This wasn't how things were supposed to go. I felt myself standing and leaning over his desk before my brain caught up with my actions.

"I am here to avenge the mutilation and humiliation of my father!" My hand went to the place where my dagger was usually kept by my side. And then I remembered that I didn't have it.

He didn't even look alarmed. In fact, his eyes darkened, and I looked down to see that my breasts were on full display leaning over his desk. I wanted to back away, but pirates didn't back away from danger. They embraced it.

He leaned forward, and I felt his minty breath against my lips.

"I thought there was to be a kiss before you ran me through?"

I hated the amusement that I heard in his voice.

"The kiss of death?" I growled out.

His lips curved up, and I felt it at the base of my stomach. This man was lethal.

And then Lily cried out, "It was my kiss!"

But Peter wasn't listening.

His eyes had narrowed to my lips, "Are you truly Hook's daughter?"

I jerked back. His words reminded me of who I was and what I had come to do.

"I can assure you. I am Captain Ebony Hook, and I am here to avenge my father!"

Peter rose to his feet. He towered over me.

"Feel free to try, Sweet Ebony, I welcome the challenge."

Clenching my hands into fists, I blurted out, "Pistols at dawn or swords?"

Peter was enjoying this entirely too much. I could see it in his eyes as they blatantly skimmed my body.

"Whichever you prefer, although to be fair, you have just taken a long journey and must be exhausted."

I was rather tired.

"Pirates don't need rest!" I blurted out, and Tink snickered.

I turned to glare at her and didn't notice that Peter had crossed from behind his desk. He gently brought my face around and tipped my chin up so that I could see his eyes.

Need and want surged through my body.

"At least get a decent meal and a good night's rest," his tone was soothing. "You are all welcome to stay at my home, until my demise, of course."

The bastard! He was making fun of me!

"I will run you through!" I demanded hotly.

He stepped closer so that there was less than an inch between us, "You are certain of that?"

"I am the best swordsman in Neverland." And I was.

He smiled, and I felt my pussy throb. This intense attraction was a nuisance.

"Then you have nothing to worry about," he purred low into my ear. "Think about your friends. They must be tired and hungry as well. Your larder is empty by now. I know that the journey is long."

He was right, damn him.

"How do I know that you won't slit my throat in my sleep?" I demanded.

He brushed a silky hair behind my ear, "I would no sooner harm a masterpiece like yourself than I would a butterfly. But, if you wish, you may arm yourself with whatever weapons or guards you deem necessary."

I thought of Alex and the lost boys.

"You will take all of us in? And give us food for the return trip?"

He nodded gravely. "It is the least I can do since you came all this way to see me."

I stuck my hand out. "Gentleman's agreement, then?"

His eyes flared as he grasped my hand. Frissons of awareness shot up my arm, and I tried to pull away, but he held me a moment longer.

"Gentleman's agreement," he concurred.

I turned to the girls and saw that Tink looked bored, and Lily a bit confused.

"You are not the boy that left," Lily murmured.

Peter turned to her, "I am sorry, Princess. But no, I am not the boy who left all those years ago. Time has a way of changing one."

He glanced at me carefully, "Perhaps you might see that during your stay here."

I bristled. "I am still going to kill you eventually. I am just seeing to the needs of my crew."

His face was impassive, but I couldn't help noting the challenge in his green eyes.

It was like a spider awaiting its prey, but I wasn't particularly certain if I was the spider or the fly.

6

PETER

My cock was rock hard. I tried not to stare at Captain Ebony Hook eating her soup. She had on this black leather corset that minimized her waist to nearly nothing. All the while, accentuating her magnificent tits. Ebony did not lack in that department.

Her dark glossy hair was thick and wavy as it carelessly fell to the middle of her back. Some of the strands covered her left eye, and I found myself wanting to push it back behind her ear.

She was a tiny little thing and resembled nothing of Captain Hook from my memories. He had tight black curls and a certain Latin flair to him. Ebony had an exotic tilt to her cheekbones and large gray eyes. I wondered who her mother could have been.

Sitting slightly further down the table was Alexander Smead. He looked more like what I would imagine Hook's progeny to look like. With black hair and a scruffy black beard, he scowled at me, not touching his food.

I was shocked to see Nibs, Cubby, and Tootles. I knew they went by different names now, much as I did. But I had never expected my past to become a part of my future.

Ebony looked up, and I felt a jolt of awareness. The woman was absolutely stunning.

"Are we to fight tonight?" she said, conversationally.

I couldn't help the smirk that formed. It was beyond adorable how bloodthirsty the creature was. I just had to remember that Ebony was used to fighting in Neverland. Where no one ever died, and people lived happily ever after.

There was no possible way that I would be fighting her, unless she wanted a good tumble in the sheets, which I was more than ready to accommodate.

"You just arrived," I said, choosing my words carefully. "You and your crew will need some time to rest and recuperate from your journey."

Her brows wrinkled, and I wanted to soothe her with my lips.

"But we wouldn't want to impose?"

Damn, she was so innocent.

"No imposition, I have plenty of room," I gestured to my home. "A few of us may need to bunk up, but it won't be unpleasant."

Tink raised her brows naughtily, "I am more than willing to share my bed."

I'LL BET SHE WAS. I hated when Tink was in human form.

"I got Tinkerbell!" Charlie shouted.

"No, I do!" Tom interjected.

"Why would she want a bunch of pussies like you two when she could have a real man," Nate winked at Tink.

Ebony seemed to be intently watching the three idiots try and take on the biggest slut I have ever known. And I have met a lot of women over the years. None of them compare to Tinkerbell.

They were in way over their heads

"Who wished you this way?" I murmured to Tink, before taking a sip of wine.

"The good Captain, of course!" Tink slipped a finger to her abundant breasts and ran it along the exposed skin.

I wasn't the least bit interested in her, so she turned her attention back to the boys.

My gaze swung to Tiger Lily. "And how do you fit into all of this?"

Her beautiful dark eyes met mine solemnly. "It was a mistake. I shouldn't have come. I thought that I would find the carefree person you once were. I was wrong."

Alexander Smead shot daggers at me.

It would appear that I had made another enemy. Although, unlike Ebony, I think he could be a problem.

"Don't say that Lily," Ebony reached a hand to cover her arm. "We have had so much fun together, haven't we?"

Tiger Lily smiled at Ebony, and I could tell she held true affection for her.

She covered Ebony's hand with her own. "We have become the best of friends. You are right, Ebony. Thank you for reminding me."

"You can still kiss him if you want," Ebony went on as I choked on my soup.

"I beg pardon?" I coughed into my napkin.

"Well, men like kissing pretty girls, don't they?"

Dear heaven above, how was I supposed to answer something like that?

My dick throbbed. I knew exactly who I wanted to kiss, and it wasn't Tiger Lily.

Ebony's cheeks began to pink, and I would have paid handsomely to find out what she was thinking at that moment.

Tiger Lily giggled, "I don't think you are supposed to ask questions like that, Eb."

Alex grunted, "Not every man wants to kiss every girl."

Ebony rounded on him. "That hasn't seemed to stop you!"

Alex turned a bright red, and Tiger Lily slumped further into her chair. I was getting the strangest impression that she had never wanted to kiss me in the first place, that this little act was more about Ebony's first mate than it was me.

"I am getting tired," Tink yawned, and a bit of pixie dust fluttered from her blonde hair.

"Of course," I removed my napkin and stood. "My housekeeper, Mrs. Worth, will be in tomorrow. I am sorry it was just soup tonight. I am not very handy in the kitchen. However, the bedrooms are already made up. So, if you will follow me, please?"

The party stood and walked down the hall with me. There were two bedrooms on this floor. The first went to Tiger Lily and Tinkerbell, and I tried to put Ebony in the next one. But she insisted that her crew were taken care of before herself.

With that in mind. Alex and Charlie took the next bedroom. We went up the stairs where Tom and Nate took the last spare room. The only other bedroom was my own.

I turned to Ebony. "I could sleep on the couch if you prefer?"

She looked at me as if trying to figure out how a man my size could fit onto the small settee. I have to admit, it would be horrible.

"No," she shook her head, "That won't be necessary. Tom and Nate have been instructed to protect me if I raise my voice at any moment. And we have a gentleman's agreement. If you are game, can I tolerate your presence for one night?"

It would be a hell of a lot more than one if I had my way. The strange thing was, I didn't have the foggiest clue if she knew what kind of danger she was really in.

I raised my hands innocently. "I won't lay a finger on you. Unless you want me too, of course."

That brow wrinkled again. "Why would I want you too?"

I shrugged. "You might need help getting out of that contraption."

I pointed to her tight corset.

She flushed. "Oh, I didn't think about that. What will I wear to sleep in?"

Nothing—or better yet, me—was my vote, but I didn't think she was ready for that.

"I can loan you a nightshirt if you wish? I only wear the bottom half anyway."

Ebony blinked her long eyelashes. "Thank you! That would be perfect."

I showed her into my bedroom and watched as she took in the massive, king-size bed and dove gray décor. It was masculine and understated next to the luxurious mahogany wood.

Her gaze went to the bathroom door, and I followed it.

"Would you like to take a shower or soak in the bath?"

Her face lit from within, "Would you mind? I know that we are not supposed to be friendly to one another. But it has been so long since I have had a hot bath!"

We would be a whole lot friendlier soon enough, I promised myself. But for the time being, I walked her into the bathroom and pulled out a plush towel. Then I leaned down to turn on the tub and noticed when I stood that her eyes were glued to my ass.

Trying not to embarrass her, I pretended not to notice. But my cock noticed.

"There is bubble bath under the counter and some lotion if you need it. Those bottles on the side are shampoo and body wash. Is there anything else you need?"

Ebony shook her head, her eyes not leaving the steaming water.

I was about to leave when she stopped me.

Please, let her ask me to join her!

"My bustier, it laces up in the back," she bit her plump lower lip, "Could you help me?"

Lifting her hair, she turned and gave me a sultry look over her shoulder.

Fuck, I might just die after all.

7

PETER

My fingers gently brushed her warm skin as I unhooked the top of the leather and I felt her shiver. Smiling, I was happy to see that she was just as affected as I was.

Ever so slowly, I untied the black ribbons and released the hook and eyelets that held her top on. I took every opportunity to touch her silky skin, relishing when I saw goosebumps appear on her arms.

My dick was inches away from her perfect ass. All I had to do was press it into her, and she would know my feelings. I couldn't have denied it.

But that damn innocence kept creeping up in the back of my mind.

She caught the leather before it fell and I stepped back, unable to take my eyes away from the broad expanse of skin. Ebony was bare from her neck to her waist, and I noticed that she hadn't needed the corset to make her tiny waist seem smaller.

When she turned around, I saw the sides of her breasts that were no longer covered by her top.

Her eyes were deep pools of gray, questioning and wanting.

"I will leave you to it," my gravelly voice made me wince.

She didn't speak, didn't blink, or even seem to breathe as I backed out of the small bathroom.

I was so fucked up. I didn't know what to do.

And then I had a fist flying at my face. I instinctively moved, grabbing the hand and whipping it behind my attacker.

Alex snarled at me, "What do you think you are doing?"

"I was showing you hospitality," I tightened my grasp, and he winced.

"I will stay with Ebony," his voice was cold. "I don't want you anywhere near her."

"It is a noble thing to protect one's sister," I guessed.

His eyes widened a fraction, betraying him, before he answered, "I don't know what you are talking about."

I took a gamble and released him. The water was shut off from inside the bathroom, and I made a motion for him to follow me. We walked in tense silence down the stairs. I showed him into my study that was far away from the guest rooms.

Without thought, I walked over to the cabinet and poured two glasses of malt whiskey. I needed something strong, with a bit of a burn.

Offering Alex one, I threw back the other.

His eyes never left my face as he sipped his own drink.

"I do not know if you share the same blood," I began, "but it is obvious that you are Hook's son."

Alex's jaw tightened. "You don't know anything."

"Why are you really here, Alex?" I sank down into my leather desk chair. "Cut the bullshit about avenging Hook. I need the truth."

Alex looked like he wanted to chop me into little pieces. We sat in silence for a moment or two, and I worried that I wasn't getting anywhere with him.

However, he did speak. "Ebony is as much my father's daughter, and I am his son."

"What does that mean?"

Alex glanced around the room taking in the rich furnishings. "He would like this, you know."

I thought of what I remembered of my old nemesis and smiled. “Not nearly ostentatious enough for the old bastard.”

Alex barked out a laugh. “You might be right about that. Look, I never anticipated that we would actually find you. Tink isn’t known on the island for her reliability. We have been gone for almost a month. Things were going according to plan, and then you showed up.”

I lifted a brow. “I do most humbly apologize, although I am not certain what for.”

Alex leaned in, offering, “My father is the cruelest man I have ever known. He left my mother without any support and Smead stepped in. He raised me like I was his own. But the older I got, the more I knew that I didn’t resemble Smead in the slightest. From what Smead has told me, they found Ebony wandering about as a small child. I don’t remember life on the ship without her. As to why Hook claimed her as his own, I have no clue. Perhaps she really is his daughter.”

“But you do not believe this to be true?” I questioned.

He shook his head. “There is too much goodness and light in Ebony. She is no more a ruthless pirate than my adoptive father was.”

“Then why does she captain the Jolly Roger?” It was as if I had too many pieces to a puzzle and couldn’t make them fit.

“I don’t know,” Alex ran a hand through his black curls. “All I know is that Hook is dying. He has grown thin and weak. His dying wish was that I take her away so that she won’t be there to see him pass.”

“That doesn’t make any sense,” I tried to reconcile this loving father with the ruthless man I knew as Hook.

Alex shrugged.

“I can answer that.”

Alex whipped his head around. “How long have you been standing there?”

Tiger Lily stepped inside the room, closing the door behind her.

"I wondered when you would join our little party," I stood and motioned for her to have a seat next to Alex.

Tiger Lily sat on the edge of her seat looking every inch of the princess that she was.

"Peter, it's good to see you." Her smile didn't reach her eyes.

"The truth, Lily, if you please," I rubbed my forehead wearily.

"Ebony is the only daughter of Long John Silver," Lily glanced at Alex apologetically. "I am sorry I lied to you. But things are much worse than you realize. Hook kidnapped Ebony from Captain Silver and tried to ransom her for dead man's chest. Something went wrong, and Silver and his crew were banished to Treasure Island forever."

"And that left Ebony with Hook?" I started to piece the mystery together. "She was valuable enough for Hook not to want any harm to come to her. Hence, he claimed the little girl as his own, knowing that you keep your friends close and your enemies (and their daughters) even closer."

Lily nodded. "As you say, Peter."

"So why did he send her away now?" Alex questioned.

"Isn't it obvious?" Lily looked at him, "Long John Silver is coming to Neverland. And Hook is scrambling. It's been years since he took her. I'd like to think that he might have some affection for Ebony, but it is more likely that he wants to save his own skin."

Alex nodded grimly, "He told me he was dying, that I was to protect her with my life. Hook said that there was no possible way that we would ever find you. I just don't understand what he could have been thinking."

It wasn't lost on me that Hook was risking his son Alex's life to save Ebony's. I wasn't sure if laughter was the appropriate response, but I chuckled just the same. The old bastard was just as wily as he always had been. Not only had he been certain they would find me, but undoubtedly he knew the day, the minute, and time they would arrive.

I smiled. "Well played Hook."

"What in the hell is that supposed to mean?" Alex looked from Lily to me and back again.

She smiled kindly at him. "That Peter will help us."

She turned to me with a knowing glance, and I sighed. That was the beauty of Hook's plan. He knew that I wouldn't be able to resist rescuing a beautiful woman in distress. Or at least my former self wouldn't have been able to. I wanted to say that I had changed. I was colder, no doubt about it. Black and white had turned into a myriad of shades for me over the years. But it seemed Hook knew me better than I did myself.

"It looks like we are returning to Neverland."

Alex fell off his chair.

8

EBONY

After a long soak in the bath, I could hardly drag myself out of the cooling water. My body felt like gelatin, and my eyes had weights glued to my eyelids that made it impossible to keep them open.

I wrapped myself in a large terry cloth towel and padded out of the bathroom and straight to Pan's large bed. He hadn't returned, and I figured that he'd decided to play the gentleman and sleep on the couch.

At this point, I wouldn't have cared if there were a dozen braggarts on the bed. I was tired and needed some rest. Slipping in between the satin sheets I moaned at how decadent they felt against my skin. I had *borrowed* a razor from Pan, and my body was silky smooth.

I promised myself I would get up in five minutes to comb out my hair and find the clothes that he'd promised to leave out.

I was fast asleep in two.

Later in the night I felt strangled by the towel and wriggled out of it, wondering why my bunk was so spacious. In my exhausted stupor, it didn't occur to me that I could be anywhere but in the Captain's quarters of the Jolly Roger.

My dreams were filled with hard muscled bodies, and hot tropical nights. I felt myself yearning for something that I didn't quite understand.

Thrashing back and forth in my sleep, I couldn't find peace. I wasn't awake enough to reason, but not asleep enough to rest.

A wall of iron clamped itself around me, whispering soothing words into my ear. With a sigh of relief, I clutched the warmth like a lifeline. I would have climbed inside of it if I could.

Finally, I slipped away into dreamland.

I FELT something hard and insistent nestled at the juncture of my thighs. My breasts were smashed against a smooth muscular chest. And my legs were entwined with someone much larger than I was.

Fuck.

I tried to shake the sleep from my mind. I was not in my berth. Memories of the club and finding Pan came flying back.

A massive arm had me trapped on top of a perfect male specimen. I glanced up hoping that I was dreaming or perhaps that one of the lost boys had gotten lonely.

I wasn't afraid of them.

Fuck.

Dark whiskers with a reddish tint coated the man's jaw.

Pan.

I wriggled to try and get out from under his arm. But the instant that I did, my pussy came in closer contact with the monster between my thighs. I bit back a moan. That felt amazing.

I glanced up again, and Pan seemed to be asleep.

Pirates were meant to explore and plunder. I reasoned and slid my legs a bit further apart so that the length of his dick touched me right where I needed it.

I shuddered in his arms.

I had never really understood sex before. No one on Neverland would ever give me the time of day. Sure, I knew what my body was capable of. But I never had elicited feelings like this from my fingers before.

I gently rocked, my eyes rolling back as the fabric of his pajama bottoms became soaked with my need.

I looked up once again, just to be certain that Pan was still sleeping, but this time I met glimmeringly hard green eyes.

"By all means," he rasped, "do continue."

I squeaked and tried to scramble off of him, but he was stronger and faster than I was.

I found our positions being flipped so that I was underneath his magnificent body.

"Don't be shy now," his gravel tone sent shivers up my spine. "You have tortured me relentlessly all night."

I opened my mouth to argue, but his lips covered any protest that I might have made.

It was a tender, exploratory kiss that I could have broken from at any moment. It was also my first kiss. I wasn't going to miss a second of it, despite the other participant being someone I was slated to kill.

He licked the seam of my lips urging me to open further, and the instant that I did a maelstrom of emotion overtook me. I was drowning in his dark taste. My stomach coiled into knots as my breasts peaked into hardened nubs.

I had no idea that passion could be this enveloping, this drugging. I couldn't help sinking my hands into his dark silky hair. The moans and groans I heard coming from my throat were nothing compared to the deep lust rising in my body.

He kissed me like he had all day to study me, and I was his favorite subject. I wanted him to feel what I was feeling. The out of control wonder that was sweeping through my body. I met his tongue with my own, gently sweeping it into his mouth and then retreating.

Pan growled, thrusting his hips forward into my open pussy.

This ratcheted up things to an entirely new level.

My hands slipped from his hair to his shoulders, feeling the breadth of their power. I felt his chest and the muscles that lined his flat stomach.

His kiss had become addictive. Every second I fell further and further under his spell until I never wanted it to stop. I desperately wanted more of his dick rubbing against that tender spot that was crying out for attention.

I thrust my hips upward and was met with him biting my lower lip.

I opened my eyes and saw that his had darkened to a terrifying degree. The next kiss was possessive. I clutched his back, my nails scraping into his skin.

His massive cock began to rhythmically rock into my pussy. I couldn't breathe. This was nothing like the mild orgasms that I knew of. I was climbing impossibly higher and higher.

My hands slipped under the fabric of his pajama pants and clutched his bare ass, and I lifted and rubbed myself shamelessly against him.

I felt his shock, but I couldn't take even a moment to register what I had done because I was flying, soaring over the precipice of pleasure. My body was shaking as he continued to thrust through the first orgasm I was ever given by another.

"Fuck," my eyes were closed, and I knew that my cum coated his pants.

Pan held himself taut above me. I could still feel his length throbbing between my legs. I didn't know what to do to help him. But I had seen Tink taking Charlie into her mouth.

I went to slip down his body, but he stopped me.

"Ebony," his dark tone coating me.

"What?" I whispered.

"I can't take advantage of you."

The words seemed to be wrenched from his lips.

"Why not?" I demanded. Wasn't I any good at this?

Shame and embarrassment flooded my body. Pan had lived on

earth for over a hundred years. There had to be countless women in his life. Why would he want to fuck an innocent who had threatened to kill him?

I tried to roll out from under him, but he wouldn't let me.

"Tell me what you are thinking?" Pan demanded, searching my face.

I knew that he would find the telling blush but prayed that he didn't guess more.

"This was a mistake," I bit off.

But my pussy throbbed in the most delightful way. It obviously didn't agree.

Pan's eyes flashed dangerously and he growled, "Tell me what is wrong!"

I closed my eyes so that I didn't have to see those green eyes staring down at me.

There was a knock at the door.

"I hate fucking house guests," Pan muttered.

I almost smiled.

"Yes?" he called out.

Alex stood on the other side, "Eb, we need to talk."

9

PETER

I had to beat one out in the shower—twice. I can't even remember how long it had been since I'd lost control like that. I can only blame it on lack of sleep and sheer insanity.

Because the moment I climbed into my bed and realized that Ebony was naked, the most carnal thoughts entered my brain. I would like to think that I am above such things. Hell, I would never get tired of her amazing body. *Who was I trying to kid?*

Her skin seemed to glow in the moonlight. Even though I have a king-size bed, there was no way I would get any sleep with a gorgeous woman inches away from me.

I got up to leave, and that was when she started mumbling in her sleep. Concerned, I waited to see if it would pass. But it only worsened. I told myself that I would wake Ebony and make her put some damn clothes on.

But when I touched her shoulder she curled into me as if finally finding home. I gritted my teeth and figured that I would wait until she fell into a deeper sleep.

That was when she crawled on top of my body, and I knew what real hell was like. Her large pillowy breasts smashed against my chest and her naked pussy straddling my cock.

I lay awake all night long. Every time I thought she might be asleep enough to move, Ebony would latch onto me like a spider monkey. Resigning myself to my fate, I closed my eyes and waited for dawn.

My cock was in pain. My head was pounding. And I had never spent a more erotic night without making love to the woman.

Then she woke up.

I feigned sleep so that she wouldn't be embarrassed by finding herself sprawled naked over a stranger.

Clearly, I underestimated her.

Ebony's tentative exploration of her body and my own was the purest form of torture. I tried to ignore it. Honestly, I did.

But when her pussy began to soak my cock through the pajama pants, something snapped.

In seconds I had her under me as I rutted at her like a teenager.

I could tell by her untutored kiss that this wasn't something she did often. For some reason, that made it all the more difficult for me to stop myself from sinking between her thighs.

Ebony had been lied to her entire life. We were on the cusp of a mission that directly involved her. The last thing she needed was to be treated like a cheap one night stand.

I grabbed a t-shirt for her, when Alex came knocking on the door, and practically shoved the both of them out after yanking it over her head. I know that I should have made sure she had underwear. But my shirt hung almost to her knees and covered a hell of a lot more than her club attire had.

Leaning my head against the shower stall, I wondered how in the hell I had fallen into my current situation.

I had no desire to fight Hook, Long John Silver, or Ebony for that matter. I had responsibilities. Hell, I owned nightclubs throughout the city of New York, Chicago, Las Vegas, and Los Angeles. I worked almost nonstop.

I couldn't just walk away and leave things to my associates.

But I couldn't let her face it all alone either.

Turning off the water, I knew that we had to move quickly.

In ten minutes I had dressed, brushed, and started down the stairs, not bothering to shave.

I walked in to see Ebony curled up in a corner of my couch. Her knees were tucked inside her shirt, and if it weren't for her just fucked hair, I would think she looked like a child.

Tink was holding court with the lost boys. I wanted to warn them that she would chew them up and spit them out. They were no match for her sexual appetite. Well, maybe the three of them together might have a chance at keeping up.

Alex sat across from Ebony, holding his head in his hands.

Lily was the only one who looked fresh as a daisy, sipping tea at the table.

"Good morning," my voice was still gruff from lack of sleep.

All the crew, except for Ebony, wished me a lukewarm greeting.

Her cheeks flushed, and I felt myself begin to grow.

Shit.

Alex stood up, "I was just explaining to Ebony that I think her father is in trouble. And that we need you to come with us back to Neverland."

Ebony narrowed her gaze, "That doesn't make any sense. Why would my father send me away if he were in trouble? Wouldn't he want me to help him?"

This is where things were going to get dicey. I wanted to tell Ebony the truth. But Alex insisted that she needed time, before we ruined everything she thought that she knew about her life.

Part of me understood what he was asking. But I had found that the truth had served me better than what was simpler at the time. However, Lily pulled rank, stating that she and Alex had known Ebony longer than I had.

Considering I had met her a few hours earlier, I had a hard time refuting their claim.

So, for now, we were doing things their way. But if at any time I felt Ebony needed to know the whole of it. I would tell her.

Their friendship be damned.

Lily set her cup back into her saucer, "Ebony, your father was merely trying to protect you. Alex is right. We need Peter to come with us to Neverland. If, once we get there, we are wrong you can just run him through."

I scowled. That hadn't been part of the plan.

Ebony wrinkled her brow. "I suppose. But why would Peter want to return to Neverland to greet his demise?"

It was a damn good question.

One that I had been asking myself repeatedly.

How could I answer that I have a savior complex that involved tiny pirate captains that seduced me in their sleep? I was in more danger living in New York City, than I was on a ship to Neverland.

Ebony wasn't from earth. She didn't have the same concepts and sense of realism that I did.

"Insanity?" I offered with a quirked brow.

Tink smirked before whispering, "I couldn't have said that better myself."

Ebony eyed me. It was the first time our eyes had met and held since I shoved her out of my bedroom.

"Will you return to Neverland with us?" she asked, quietly.

I nodded.

"I need your word that you will not harm me or any member of my crew."

I grit my jaw. If one of my business associates questioned my integrity, they would be lying flat on the floor with a black eye.

I walked over to her, holding out my hand to shake. "I, Peter Gallagher, swear to bring no harm to Captain Ebony Hook or her crew on the Jolly Roger."

"Who in the hell is Peter Gallagher?" Alex flew up from his seat.

This was going to take a while.

10

EBONY

Peter Pan had been living on earth as Peter Gallagher. My father was in trouble and hadn't told me. And here is the real kicker, somehow, I had been convinced that bringing Peter back to Neverland was the way to save my father.

He claimed insanity. I think I have the corner share of that one locked up right and tight.

I still felt like I was walking about in a daze as we loaded up Peter's things, as Peter made whatever business arrangements he needed to take care of his nightclubs while we were gone. At long last, Tinkerbell sprinkled us with pixie dust to return to the ship.

The rest of my crew looked at Peter warily and I had to admit, I didn't blame them. He was huge and rather intimidating even in brown trousers and a leaf green pullover.

I couldn't help staring at him. Perhaps it was because his eyes matched his shirt making them bright against his tan skin, or because he had a body that rivaled a hardened sailor's.

Or maybe, it was just me.

"Where do you want to put him?" Alex huffed. "We have no spare cabins or berths."

"String up a hammock somewhere," I waved him off.

Honestly, I was preparing for another long voyage. Surely, Alex could take care of such a simple task.

Tiger Lily had been distant ever since we'd found Peter. I knew that she had wanted to kiss him, but the very thought had my blood boiling. There was no way in hell she was putting her lips anywhere near him.

And no, I didn't want to evaluate that further.

Preparing to leave was always hard work which left little time for discussion. What I hadn't expected was that Peter would jump in and work alongside us.

I even saw Alex give him a look of approval when he helped with the sails of the mizzen mast.

Perhaps, things were looking up.

We worked almost twenty-four hours straight, sailing out of earth's atmosphere and breaking back into outer space.

Peter taught us all kinds of things about oxygen and how what we were doing was completely impossible. I couldn't believe the rubbish that he was spouting about needing fresh air and how we should have burnt up as we crossed.

Apparently, Peter could be very dramatic.

When things settled, we were able to leave the less complicated navigating to my crew. I trudged down the stairs to my cabin.

I had been wearing a corset that closed in the front. Without thought, I kicked off my boots and unlaced the black leather. My skin welcomed the fresh breeze that gently raised goosebumps and puckered my nipples.

With a sigh of relief, I tossed my clothing to the side, having already removed my pants, I began to brush my teeth. I had a mouth full of toothpaste when my cabin door was thrust open and Peter stood in the doorway.

It took him a second and a half, before he swiftly slammed the door behind him.

"Good Lord, woman! Do you ever wear clothes?" he growled at me.

I spit the toothpaste out, trying to not show how much his presence discomposed me.

"I always sleep nude," I replied loftily.

His eyes darkened.

"Why are you here?" I blurted out, not sure if I should sit or stand. I had never been trained on naked etiquette. Does one just stand there? Surely, not?

"This is my room," he returned silkily.

I put my hands on my hips, only belatedly noticing how it made my boobs jut out towards him.

"This is the Captain's Quarters, and you are not the captain."

His eyes were glued to my body and for a moment I thought he wouldn't respond.

"Erm," I cleared my throat.

He lazily brought his gaze to mine. "You told Alex to find a place to hang my hammock. He said that I could damn well do that myself. This is where I chose."

Sure enough, in the far corner of my room was a hammock swinging with the sway of the ship.

"Hell, no." I stamped my foot causing way too much of my body to jiggle.

His voice was thick and husky. "Fuck, yes."

"Bastard!" I snarled.

He was on me in a second, all heat and hard body, as he pressed me against the wall.

"I never claimed to be anything more," he bit the side of my neck, making me moan through clenched teeth.

"Get off me," I demanded, but it came out as more of a breathy plea.

"Not a chance," his warm lips grazed the shell of my ear, and I felt my heart gallop out of my chest. My stomach had sunk to my toes, and my brain had abandoned me. Nothing was where it was supposed to be. Least of all him.

"Peter," I had meant to sound stern, but by the way he growled when I said his name, I knew I had failed miserably.

Then he kissed me.

All thought of escaping or beating him over the head with the nearest object was replaced by his sinful mouth.

My hands clutched his shirt as I rose onto my tiptoes to better reach him.

He slanted his mouth, forcing me to open mine. I couldn't believe I was doing this…again. I had told myself after the night in his bed that I would steer clear of Peter.

The feelings that enveloped me whenever he was near scared the living daylights out of me.

I found myself doing things and making decisions that made me wonder if he had drugged me.

The way his lips moved against mine was certainly intoxicating. I wanted more. No, I needed more. Wrapping my arms around his neck I leapt up, and he caught me as my legs coiled about him.

There was never any break from the kiss. It was as if he knew what I needed and was one step ahead of me.

Being this close to his hard body, I couldn't help relishing the way my nipples felt as they grazed against his shirt, my body grinding against his, in the most shameless manner.

He wrenched his lips away as he laid me on my berth, "You are like holding fire. I know I am going to get burned, but I am fascinated by the flame."

I smiled in the fashion of women since the beginning of time. "Can't handle it, Pan?"

He ripped his shirt off and my jaw dropped.

Next, he removed his shoes and pants until all he wore were thin cotton briefs.

His dick was so large that the mushroomed head poked a bit out of the top of his underwear.

"Fuck," I panted, "Is it supposed to be that massive?"

His eyes narrowed, "What is that supposed to mean?"

"It's just that I have never seen one," I swallowed nervously, "Stretched out like that."

He stalked me like a panther does its prey.

"Are you trying to say that you have never seen a man's erect cock before?"

I shook my head, cheeks blushing, "I mean I saw Tinkerbell sucking off Charlie once."

"Holy fuck! You need a keeper," he growled, hopping onto the bed but keeping his dick away from me. "How did I end up with a virgin?"

I blinked. Not sure if he meant that in a good way or a bad way.

"Just lucky I guess." I tried smiling, but it fell short.

He blew out a shuddering breath. "Lucky, indeed."

11

PETER

Never in my life have I ever been faced with such temptation. Ebony's heavy-lidded eyes followed my every move. The girl should never play poker. Every thought written across her gorgeous features was clear for me to read.

She wanted me.

And I sure as hell wanted her.

I leaned over and captured her lips in a lingering kiss. I wanted to know every inch of her mouth by the taste and touch of mine. She moaned deep in her throat.

The sounds she made had my gut clenching, and my heart rocketing about its cage. She bit my lip, and I nearly came undone.

I pulled back to kiss her eyelids, her forehead and then trailed kisses along her jawline. Ebony writhed beneath me, tilting her head to the side so that I had better access.

Everything about her was liquid sensuality. Ebony was effortlessly taking to lovemaking as a duck did to water.

My need for her was growing exponentially with every catch of her breath, every involuntary shudder.

Her hands roamed my chest but hadn't ventured out further. I wanted her to feel me, to not be afraid. Gently I took one of her hands and wrapped it around my cock. We both hissed at the contact.

I took her hand in mine and showed her what I liked, what I needed.

Ebony's gray eyes looked dark and hooded. "Touch me," she said softly, and I took her breasts into my hands.

I was fascinated by how my tan skin looked against the pale globes. Her magnificent breasts were no longer smashed into a corset, and after seeing them like this, I almost wished they could always be mine.

But that would be ridiculous, and I shoved the thought away.

I took her nipple into my mouth, sucking, and flicking it with my tongue. Ebony was incredibly sensitive, and I knew with every suck that her pussy was getting wetter. I switched to the other side and made sure that it got the same exquisite attention.

Her hands were tightening on my dick as she arched her back, trying to shove her tits further into my mouth.

I broke away and looked down at her. "We can still stop."

I was panting like a madman. My hair, no doubt, was standing on end from her fingers, and my body was poised on the brink.

But I didn't want to take anything from her that she wasn't willingly giving away.

"Fuck me, Peter," her whisper went straight to my dick, and my heart seized in my chest.

I knelt in front of her, spreading her thighs wide. The scent of her arousal washed over me, and I knew I needed a taste.

Lifting her hips to my face, I kept my green eyes locked on her gray ones.

Languidly, I licked her entire pussy in long strokes. Her hands flew to her breasts and began to squeeze them.

"Play with your nipples, Ebony," I instructed. "Show me what feels good."

Her face lit with color, but she did as she was told. Her small fingers, drawing tight circles around her nipples until they were aching and hard.

I continued to eat her pussy like it was a gourmet meal and I was on death row.

I lapped up her honeyed juices and used my fingers to try and help ease into her tight hole.

She gasped when I put two fingers into her. Her fingers were pulling harshly on her nipples. I watched her every movement to be sure that she was getting the greatest pleasure from me.

A third finger made it incredibly tight. And my dick wept, knowing how amazing she was going to feel.

I sucked her clit into my mouth, rhythmically pulling, as her hips thrashed, and she released for me, shuddering as beautifully as an angel.

I didn't want her to feel pain, but I had waited long enough.

My dick demanded to be inside of her.

I held it in my hands and coated the head with her cum. Ebony's eyes flashed with desire, and I knew I couldn't wait any longer.

Sliding the tip inside, I gasped at the tightness that threatened to have me spilling like a youth.

"Fuck," I willed my body to hold still, wanting her to get used to the fullness.

I pushed a little further in. "Open your eyes, Ebony, and don't close them."

Her gray eyes popped open, and I saw so many conflicting emotions there that it startled me. But the greatest of all was need, and I could do something about that.

I slid an inch further. The process was long and arduous and ultimately the most fantastic experience of my life.

"I am sorry," I whispered. "I don't want to hurt you."

A tear slipped down her cheek, and I felt it everywhere.

"Do you want me to stop?"

To be honest, I wasn't sure that I could. But I would try, for her.

"No," she winced. "Just give me a second."

I leaned down and kissed her again. Deep drugging kisses that would take her mind off the pain. My dick felt like it was caught in a vise. I wasn't sure it had ever felt this good before.

Her hips began to move, and I sank to the hilt. It was, by far, the best thing I had ever experienced. I couldn't wait any longer.

Pulling out slowly, I thrust my hips back again, sinking until I was completely enveloped by her heat. It felt so fucking good.

Back and forth I gently glided, not wanting to hurt her and desperate to plunge with abandon. I keep my moves measured and calm. Her juices began flowing again, and it was easier to thrust. Her hips began meeting mine.

"Yes!" I growled out. Pushing harder, going deeper, relishing every moan, as she climbed her way to ecstasy once more.

I was on the brink, but I wasn't going to spend it without her.

Reaching between us, I rubbed her engorged clit. It stood out proud and fuck if that wasn't sexy as hell.

Her gray eyes rolled back as her body finally broke. I quickly thrust into her, making the most of every contraction, drawing out her orgasm and bringing mine closer.

At the last moment, I pulled out and spent on her tight stomach.

"Fuck, Ebony, you were incredible."

She was panting, trying to catch her breath, "That," she closed her eyes, "Nobody said it would be like that."

I stood and grabbed a towel to wipe her stomach. But her words stayed with me.

"Do you mean that in a good way or a bad way?" I hated the hesitation in my voice, but the question had to be asked.

I crawled into the small berth next to her. There was just enough room for us if we lay closely together.

Ebony went one further and entangled her legs with mine, laying her head in the crook of my neck.

"In a fucking fantastic way," she muttered, sleepily.

Then I remembered that we hadn't rested for over twenty-four hours. I pulled her naked body tighter against my own.

"Sleep, Little One."

She made a face but was too exhausted to reply.

I lay awake for a while watching her in the moonlight. I felt different, changed somehow. All I could think of was that a pirate's daughter from Neverland wouldn't want to live in the corporate world.

I had fucked this up. But now that I had tasted Ebony, I didn't think I could let her go.

Hook would certainly never understand, and I had never met Silver. But from what I understood, he was much more ruthless. It was late into the night before I finally succumbed to sleep. I dreamt of pirate ships, sword fights, and mayhem, but mostly I dreamt of her.

12

EBONY

The air in the hold was rancid and putrid. Even on a magical pirate ship people get seasick and the heat becomes oppressive.

The only tolerable location is on the deck, where the wind caresses your overheated body and the air smells a bit like sunlight. The crew had stripped down to the least amount of clothing that they could get away with. At least, without me throwing them overboard.

I was used to the state of undress of my crew and had even accustomed myself to Lily and the Lost boys. Tink was always dressed in next to nothing so no adjustment was necessary there.

Peter, on the other hand, was a constant distraction. My eyes would catch the muscles rippling in this back. His pants, which had become looser from the physical exertion, hung so low on his hips that I could see the dimples above his ass.

I wanted to lick them. Feel them with my fingertips as he thrust his gigantic cock inside of me. More than once someone had to clear their throat to gain my attention. It was humiliating.

To make matters worse, he had left my cabin the morning after our tryst. Peter tried to ignore me and was successful a good deal of the time. However, when I decided what was good for the goose was good for the gander, I exchanged my corset for a black lacy bra that was three times too small.

I had been out of my cabin for approximately twelve seconds when I found myself thrown over a strong male's shoulder and hauled back in.

"Are you insane?" Peter raged as he tossed me onto the bed.

I coughed politely and enquired innocently, "What are you talking about?"

"Your damn nipple is hanging out for hell's-sake Ebony!"

I looked down and indeed my right breast seemed to be crawling out of the tight bra.

"What is a little nip-slip between friends?" I ventured.

He pounced on me. His hard, sweaty body covered mine as his teeth grazed my nipple.

Holy Fuck!

"Your body is mine!" Peter growled, "You are not showing it to all of the dumb shits on board. Damn it, Eb, are you trying to get hurt?"

I drew back. "No one can harm me! I am the Captain!"

He pressed into me. "Fine, if you are so damn sure, fight me off."

I scowled, trying to ignore the heat of his breath skimming my ear.

"I am not fighting you."

"Okay," his body relaxed, and I felt his weight cutting off my oxygen.

"Shit, Peter, I can't breathe! Get off!" I shoved against his rock-hard chest.

"I'm tired," he feigned a yawn, "I think I will take a nap."

"You shithead, I can't fucking breathe!"

Peter turned his head. "Then fight."

I squirmed underneath him, pushing him with all my strength. Peter didn't move an inch. Well, his frame didn't. But I felt his cock begin to lengthen.

He raised himself to his elbows. "Oh, Ebony! I didn't realize you were down there."

"Hardy-har-har," I griped. "What are you trying to prove?"

His smile tugged at my gut."I think my point has been made."

"You think you want to get laid?" I quipped, "Peter, this is so forward of you!"

His eyes darkened to an emerald green. "You are pushing it, Little One."

I reached down between us and grabbed his cock. "I like the push and pull."

Perhaps I was playing with fire, maybe I was bored, or quite possibly I was finally giving in to the chemistry that had been brewing around us the last few days.

"You and I," he shook his head, "There can't be an us."

I tried not to flinch at his words. I wasn't stupid. I knew the complications as well as he did.

"Why did you say that I was yours then?" I snapped.

He clenched his jaw.

"I don't belong to you or anyone else. This here, it's just a bit of fun. When all is said and done I am not expecting a ring. Shit, Peter, I'm a pirate. If I want to fuck half the crew, you can't do anything about it."

His face turned to pure rage, "You will not fuck anyone else!"

"It's my body." I was hurt and spouting off anything I could to make him feel the same way. "You aren't the only cock on board if you don't want me."

"Don't want you?" he barked incredulously. "You are insane!"

His lips ravaged mine, there was nothing gentle about this kiss. It was all tongues and gnashing of teeth as he plundered my depths. The immediate response of my body wasn't lost on me. My heart thundered in its cage and I felt the tight coil of need awaken in my belly.

He bit my lip and I bit him back, it was tit for tat and I wasn't about to lose this one.

Hiking my leg around his hips, I thrust myself against his heat.

He flipped our positions so that I was straddling him. His hands snapped the offending bra in half and he tossed it away from the bed.

Then he brought his lips up to my peak and sucked. I cried out his name, pushing more of my breast into his mouth. He loosened his grip on my hips and I had my chance.

Jerking my lips away, I flew off the berth.

"Looks like I got away from you," I taunted as my chest heaved up and down.

I was struggling to draw air into my lungs. Or maybe I was just so aroused that I needed a moment to collect myself.

Peter didn't have the same needs because I found myself slammed against the wall of my cabin.

My legs automatically wrapped about his waist and I clung to his naked shoulders.

"What are you doing?" I squeaked.

"You can't get away from me, Ebony," Peter nipped at my neck. "You can run all you want, but I will always be right behind you."

I was going to tell him something snappy about that sounding stalkerish, but he claimed my lips again and my mind turned to mush.

I clung to him, savoring the smell of his hard body next to mine. It should have been awful. We were both hot and sweaty. But he smelled of the ocean and raw masculinity.

I ground my core against his dick, willing him to take the next move, but he seemed content to just kiss me.

There was a pounding on the door before Tiger Lily barged in.

"Ebony, we have trouble…"

She broke off her sentence as a knowing smile crossed her face.

"You don't like him, huh?"

I could have killed her in cold blood.

"Not even a little bit," I said as haughtily as I could. It was impossible to appear cold and unaffected when I was smashed between Peter and the wall.

"And you don't care if I get that kiss?" she teased.

"You fucking touch one inch of Peter and I will tell Alex what you say in your sleep."

Lily's face flooded with color. "That is low, Ebony."

Peter's lips twitched. "And why are you here?"

She straightened angrily and retorted, "Pirate ship off the port bow."

"In space?" I blurted out.

"Fuck." Peter dropped me on the floor.

13

EBONY

"Explain to me again why Tiger Lily is pretending to be me, and why I am supposed to be her?"

I sat gussied up in Tiger Lily too tight clothes as she glided around the deck doing a damnably good impression of me. The pirate ship was approaching at a steady clip. But they didn't have their cannons out.

This was the strangest day I had ever had.

"I already told you," Alex sighed. "Their ship is three times the size of ours Eb. If we put up a fight, we all die. And besides that, salient point, Long John Silver has a bone to pick with Hook. If we let him take you, we will never see you again."

"But you are willing to part with Tiger Lily?" I fired back, my eyes not leaving the massive ship approaching. They had the skull and crossbones waving in the breeze.

Alex clenched his jaw, and I knew he was trying to reign in his temper.

"No, I am not happy with that. But my vote was overruled. I wanted to send Tinkerbell in your stead."

"I heard that!" Tink called out, from where she was flirting with Tom.

"I meant you to," Alex replied sneakily.

Tom growled at Alex.

"Stop," I put my hand up, but Tiger Lily was already on it.

Getting right in Alex's face she yelled, "You are not helping. Stop being a dumb-fuck and try being useful."

Shit.

She did know me.

Alex flushed, "Sorry, Captain."

He has never been that respectful to me in all the years that I have known him.

Alex had it bad for Tiger Lily. I just didn't understand why he didn't go for her. Didn't she seem to like him back?

Not that I was an expert in romance. Clearly, a novice, but one plus one still equals two in my book.

"Ahoy there!" There was a loud cry from the other ship, and we braced ourselves, guns at the ready just in case. "We mean you no harm, friends."

Pirates don't have friends.

There was a sizable creaking sound and then a jolt where we almost lost our footing as the ships came alongside each other. This captain defied description. He had a wooden leg and carried a crutch that he brandished about when he spoke.

A large parrot perched on his shoulder. He was a giant of a man, limber and quick with sparkling eyes.

"Well now, aren't you a hearty crew! Is this my old friend Hook's vessel? I dare say, I never thought the Jolly Roger would be manned by anyone but the old crook."

I felt myself bristle and went to retort when Alex elbowed me in the stomach.

"My father," Tiger Lily replied with as much pride and circumstance as a queen.

They were never going to believe this.

"Ebony?" his voice cracked and strangely enough, I felt it clear through my bones.

"Yes," she replied, folding her arms across her chest.

"Tis me, Sweetness, your pa. I am Long John Silver, and you are my sweet Ebony."

What the actual fuck was going on?

"My father is Captain Hook," Tiger Lily didn't miss a beat. But my eyes were glued to Captain Silver.

"Sweet Ebony! Squawk!"

"Ai, Captain Flint, it is our little girl, returned to us at last."

"Are you addressing the bird?" I asked without thinking. Alex sent me a thunderous glare.

Long John Silver grinned. "This here is Captain Flint. He sails the seas with me and has for many a year."

"What happened to the original Captain Flint?" Peter came out from the shadows and Silver's eyes narrowed.

"Strapping young lad, now aren't you? That's a fine question and one that I have an excellent answer to!"

"You tell 'em, Barbeque!" One of his sailors called out.

"Barbeque?" I repeated dumbly.

"Tis on account that I used to be the Quartermaster, but it's been nigh on a hundred years since those days," Silver smiled again at Tiger Lily.

"We just came to get you darlin.' If you come along with us, we won't harm your friends."

"You can't take her!"

I shoved my way past Alex and out into the light.

Silver's breath caught in his throat. It was as if he had seen a ghost.

"You are the spitting image of her," his genial tone falling away as honesty prevailed. "It's been so long since I laid eyes on the both of you."

I felt a strange churning in my stomach. "What are you speaking of, Pirate? State your case and then be gone. We need to return to my father. He is ill."

"I know what be ailing Hook," Silver's eyes glinted. "But he's not your father, Sweetness. Why did you send another girl before? What trickery is this? Did you think I wouldn't know my own? I have her likeness. I carry it with me everywhere. Would you like to see your mother, child?"

I took a step forward only to have a large hand yank me backward.

"You are going to be the death of me," Peter hissed. He walked over and grabbed a rope. Pushing off with his legs, he swung over the side onto the other ship.

"I will bring it to her," Peter growled.

Silver tipped his head to the side. "Do you I know you, lad? There is something about your eyes that is rather familiar."

Peter cocked a brow, "Do you find yourself involved with the club scene in Manhattan?"

"Liar, Squawk," chimed in Captain Flint.

Peter snarled at the bird.

"Don't mind him," Silver cajoled. "Can't say I have ever been much of a dancer."

He motioned to his peg leg, and I snorted a laugh.

It was rude, but I couldn't help it. An answering smile crossed Silver's face as he reached into his pocket and pulled out a silver locket.

"Did I miss anything?" Tink and Tom rejoined us on the deck. "Oh, Silver! How lovely to see you again!"

The captain's eyes flew from Tink to Peter and back again.

"Well, well, if it isn't Peter Pan all grown up." All the friendliness had evaporated, and Silver sounded like the bloodthirsty pirate he undoubtedly was.

"Oops!" Tink covered her broad smile with a hand.

Peter went to swing away but was stopped by five of Silver's crew.

"Don't run away on me now," Silver stroked his whiskered chin. "I have much I wish to discuss with you."

Peter's jaw clenched, "As you wish, Captain."

Silver looked over to where I was standing on the deck of the Jolly Roger. And again, his expression softened for the briefest of moments.

"Take the lot!" He commanded harshly. In the next second, there were dozens of sailors swinging onto the Jolly Roger.

We fought with skill and determination. Swords were clashing as they met again and again. I swung my saber with my right hand while using my dagger to stab with the left.

I saw Charlie go down, but there wasn't much blood, so I had hopes that he would be fine.

Tom was leading his tormentor on a merry chase up the rigging while Alex wielded his weapon bravely.

There were just so many of them. I wanted to be proud of the fight my crew was putting up. And I was, for the most part. Tink had disappeared once again, and there was no sign of Nate. I was going to wish her small, at my earliest convenience.

They trounced us in about eight minutes.

It was dismal, to say the least.

"Bring my daughter over here!" Silver called out as if asking for another spot of tea, not a person.

I was grabbed by a burly character. I kicked my feet and bit him, at least seven times. But it was to no avail. And with a gruff hold, we were airborne and sailing towards the larger vessel.

Can I help that my heart was grateful Peter was already on board? Perhaps Alex wasn't the only one who had it bad.

14

PETER

I eyed Silver's crew with a hint of trepidation, wondering who would recognize the little boy in the man I had become.

Black Dog, Billy Bowlegs, Iron hand, Ned Shill and all the rest looking as grungy as ever. It had been far too long, and I could have gone a lifetime more.

The Henrietta was a fine ship, far more extensive than The Jolly Roger. Hook had stolen the name of the pirate flag for his ship. His lack of originality wreaked of amateurism; Hook was never meant to be a pirate Captain.

Dodd Perch was his real name. He faked a big death scene, and Captain James Bartholomew Hook was born.

But I supposed we all wore masks of some kind, so who was I to point fingers?

My arms were tied behind my back, and they had secured my feet with rope. But I could still speak.

"Captain Silver, surely we can come to some type of arrangement?"

Silver turned to where I was standing. Black Dog had Ebony as she fought tooth and nail to be free of him. These weren't the type of pirates that Ebony knew. Her fairytale existence was about to come to a crashing halt.

"You always did have a silvery tongue, Jim."

Fuck.

Ebony ceased all movement. "Who is Jim?"

I had hoped she wasn't paying attention to our conversation.

"That there is Jim," Silver smiled, and I wanted to knock his teeth out. "Jim Hawkins and I have a history, don't we son?"

"I am not your son," I bit off.

His grin widened. "You see, Sweet Ebony, Jim here took on the name of Peter Pan when he and Dodd Perch stole Captain Flint's treasure."

"Who is Dodd Perch?" Ebony blinked in confusion.

"Your father," Alex blurted out, "Or rather, Hook."

We all swung round to face Alex.

"Smead told me the whole thing one night over a bottle of rum," Alex went on bitterly. "Told me that I wasn't his, as much as he loved me, but a cast-off of Dodd's. I didn't understand until later who he was referring to. But at another date, I heard Smead slip up and call Hook by his real name."

"Why has everyone changed their names?" Ebony demanded, "This doesn't make any sense."

Silver's laugh rumbled out of his chest. "She is as bright as a penny! You see, darlin,' when a pirate steals from another pirate they become the walking dead. Dead men don't bite, is what they used to say. So, by assuming new names they think they have outrun their past. But they haven't, have they, Jim?"

I was tense. "My name is Peter. It was never Jim Hawkins. I made that up when I came on your ship. My given name is Peter Gallagher, and that is the name I go by to this day. I am positive your mother didn't christen you Long John Silver."

In a flash, a long saber was thrust in the direction of my throat. I dodged, half expecting a hothead like Silver to try something similar.

Ebony screamed, "Do not touch him! Do you understand me?"

Silver turned to her, a curious glint in his eye. "Now tell me, lass, why you are so attached to *Peter* here and perhaps I will spare his life."

He was bluffing. Silver wouldn't dispatch me so quickly. There was much more to reveal, and he needed what resided in my brain.

"He's," She swallowed, her chest rising and falling with fear as Black Dog held her immovable. "He's my husband. And if you truly are my father, you won't harm the man I love."

Her declaration sent a shock wave through the crew.

My heart was pounding a million miles a minute. I couldn't refute her, and the Lord knew that I wanted it to be true. But I couldn't help but feel an ominous warning that this could only end badly.

Silver whipped his gaze back to me, and I tried to remain impassive.

Tink looked incredulous, and that was nothing compared to Alex whose chin was dangling somewhere near his knees.

"I don't believe you," Silver declared after a moment of speculation.

I thought it might be a good idea to say something here, but I hadn't the slightest idea what to add.

It turns out. It was Tiger Lily who saved us.

"They are married, Captain Silver. I have witnessed them being alone together. They behave as all newly married couples do."

Ebony's cheeks heated, and I scowled.

"You married my little girl?" Silver got right into my face, and I could smell the rancid meat he had eaten earlier.

"She is mine," was my only response.

Silver swung his beefy fist, connecting with my jaw.

"Stop!" Ebony cried out. But Silver had only just gotten started.

Crack, the next punch split my lip and the next blackened by eye. I had known the chance I was taking, getting involved with her. I could take the consequences, but Ebony was not of the same frame of mind.

She bit Black Dog and shimmied under his arms as he jerked

away from her. Grabbing another pirate's sword, she brandished it like a pro.

"You will stop this instant!" she screamed. "Or I will run you through."

Silver was winded from the exertion. "He took my little girl away from me!"

"I am not a little girl. I am a grown woman. And if you were my father, you would respect my wishes."

"I AM YOUR FATHER!"

Silver yanked out the silver locket that he had stashed in his front pocket. Ebony took it from Silver's dirty hands and opened the lock. Her lower lip trembled, and her eyes began to swim with tears.

I wanted to go to her, comfort her. But as much as I strained against the ropes, I couldn't budge.

Slowly, Ebony turned it around so that I could see the likeness inside. The woman's hair was done in an old-fashioned style. Her clothing reflected a time long since passed. But for those discrepancies, it could very well have been Ebony. She had the same wispy hair that looked like hazelnuts, the same sparkling eyes, and cupid's bow mouth.

"Damn it," I muttered.

She nodded jerkily. "I will listen to what you have to say."

Silver's smile could be seen for leagues around. However, it dimmed when Ebony finished her statement.

"But I will need my husband free from the restraints and my crew treated as guests, not prisoners."

Some of Silver's crew spouted off what they thought Ebony could do with her requests. But Silver ignored their banter and focused his attention on Ebony.

"Will you listen to everything I have to say with an open heart?"

Ebony nodded, "I give you my solemn vow."

Silver's eyes gleamed. "Release the prisoners!"

Ebony cleared her throat rather loudly.

Silver looked sheepish, "Right! Release the *guests* and show them to their new chambers. We will have some crew go back to the Jolly Roger to man the wheel."

"Where are we headed?" Ebony asked Silver.

He laughed, "To Neverland, it's the second star to the right and straight on till morning."

I felt the ropes loosen around my feet and then again at my back. I barely had enough time to bring them around as Ebony launched herself into my arms.

"I'm sorry," she whispered in my ear, and I felt a flood of emotion fill my heart.

Her tender lips against my flesh had me shivering with need. I held her tighter to me. She had no reason to be sorry. We should have been more forthright with her. I should have been more forthright despite Alex's protests.

I had a feeling that things were only starting to become complicated, and we were nowhere near in the clear yet.

15

EBONY

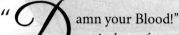

"Damn your Blood!"

A shout from one of the sailors awakened me from my slumber.

I was about to fall back to sleep when another voice cried out, "I come from hell and I will carry you there presently!"

The first sailor seemed to take offense to this and retorted, "I'll cut you in pound pieces!"

"Not before I pull out your bleeding heart!" It sounded like it was followed by the brandishing of a sword.

"You'd both better bloody well shut your mouths, before I cut out your tongues," I yelled from the hammock I had dozed off in.

Both sailors looked over to see that I was indeed awake and not amused.

"Beg pardon, Captain Hook," this came from Brownie who was one of my better midshipmen.

"Sorry, Ma'am," Billy Bowlegs made an awkward bow mixed with a salute.

I felt someone's presence near my side and turned to see Peter staring at me.

"If there is something on my face I would prefer you tell me now." My face heated as I tried to sit up gracefully.

The hammock had other ideas and began to twist to the right as I slid to the left and the next thing I knew my ass was smacking the floor.

"Go ahead and laugh," I dared him, brandishing my dagger that I'd ripped from my boot.

Peter's lips did not so much as twitch. However, his eyes danced.

"I wouldn't dream of it." He extended a hand and I took it gratefully. "I don't know why you insisted on sleeping up here when you have a perfectly good bunk in a private cabin."

I wrinkled my nose in distaste. The room below was dank and dark, nothing like the captain's quarters that I was used to. To be perfectly honest, it made me uncomfortable.

I supposed I should have been happy to not be bunking with the crew, but it wasn't the luxury of my cabin that I was used to. Alex and Lily were tasked with the crew to fly the Jolly Roger, but Silver insisted that Peter and I remain aboard the Henrietta.

"I like the fresh air," I said loftily, releasing my arm from his strong grasp.

He nodded. "Yes and sleeping on the deck of the ship apparently. It's a good thing it doesn't get chilly out here in space."

"You are being an ass-hat," I scowled when his broad chest began to shake with laughter.

"You know as well as I do that it is freezing on deck. Your fingers were so cold when I helped you up that I worried they might break off."

I sighed and attempted to casually shoved my frost-bitten hands into my armpits. It was a dismal failure as his eyes watched my every move. "It is cold as fuck out here in space. I have on three layers already. It is hard to imagine that last week when we joined Silver we were complaining about the heat."

Peter pulled my hands out and held them in his large warm ones. I felt tingles all the way down to my toes. It could have been that they were finally getting blood circulating through them. But I liked to think that it had something to do with Peter.

"Why won't you sleep downstairs?" he asked again, quieter this time. "I know that you are not sleeping at night. You have dark circles around your eyes that look like bruises. You need your sleep, Ebony."

"This is a lot to take in," I blurted out. "Everything I thought I knew about myself and those around me is a lie. I don't know who to trust. Shit, I don't even trust myself."

Peter pulled me into his chest. His body heat brings life back to my frozen limbs.

"You are like an ice cube, Eb," it was said under his breath and sadly coincided with a loud sneeze from yours truly. "We are going to your cabin!"

He scooped me up and carried me. I didn't fight Peter. I knew that I was tired. But the moment we went into the dark cabin I felt that awful claustrophobia starting to creep back in.

"I can't stay here," I grumbled, squirming.

"Ebony, why the hell not?" he ran a hand through his hair after setting me on my feet.

"I-don't-feel-comfortable." I blurted.

"Ebony, was that an answer or a sneeze?"

I grabbed his arms for support, "I don't feel comfortable here. It is too dark, the room smells, and I hear scratching that I am positive is rats."

"Most ships have rats, Eb. Even the Jolly Roger has been known to carry a few."

I knew that.

I wasn't stupid.

"But never inside of my cabin," I said in a low voice.

Peter sighed, "What if someone stayed with you?"

"You will?" I grabbed him around the waist and squeezed with all of my might. "Thank you, Peter, thank you!! You won't regret it, I promise."

I knew that he intended to put someone else in here, but the truth was that if it wasn't going to be Alex or Tiger Lily, it had to be him. And if I am truthful I only wanted him. I wanted to feel his naked skin brush against my own.

I wanted him to kiss me until I forgot all about fathers and kidnapping and, most of all, treasures. I wanted someone in this universe to want me for me, and not what I could do for them.

I gathered, from what everyone has said, that Hook only took me in so that he could use me as leverage later, against my natural father. Silver only wanted me so that he could force Hook to reveal where he'd buried the treasure that he'd stolen from Silver when I was kidnapped as a young child.

I was even questioning my relationship with Alex. He did care for me, I knew that. But how much of our friendship was based on him trying to gain the attention and affection of his natural father? All these thoughts plagued me at night in the dark.

"Please do not make me stay here alone," the whispered plea was low, and I internally cursed the needy note in my tone.

Peter's strong arms wrapped around me, "If you want me, I will stay with you."

I looked up to see his green eyes looking at me intently. He scooped me up and placed me into the berth of the small room.

"I will be right back," Peter kissed my forehead. "Do not move."

I nodded and watched as his broad back walked out of the space. I had started shivering again and prayed that I wasn't getting sick. The cold of space had seeped into my bones and wrapped itself so tight that I felt I would never be warm again.

The door opened, and Peter entered along with Tinkerbell.

Her nose wrinkled, "This is terrible!"

I had seen the other cabins and knew it was as good or better than most, but I couldn't comment with my teeth clattering together.

Peter gave Tink a pointed look, and she sighed before conjuring up some fairy dust. She sprinkled it everywhere. Along the walls over the floors and even the bed.

My jaw unclenched when I felt warmth begin to settle around me. In a flash, I realized that I had never been this cold on my ship.

"What did you do?" I asked.

Tink shrugged, "I just sealed the cabin of leaks. Your blankets are fuller and your pillows softer. I can't fix everything, but I can make it bearable."

"Did you do this for everyone?" I had to ask.

Tink blushed, "Those not fairy born, fairies don't really feel the cold. Our hearts burn like fires, I know it sounds strange, but they keep us very warm. Most don't enjoy our touch because of how hot we are."

She placed a hand on my arm to show me and I almost threw myself into her arms.

"You are so warm, Tink!" I soaked in every ounce of heat she was willing to give.

She wriggled out of my grasp, "Hook had me do this on his ship eons ago. I suppose I should have remembered when we came aboard the Henrietta."

"Tink, you enjoy being human-sized, do you not?" I asked carefully. I needed her on my side.

She nodded cautiously.

"How do you think that Silver is able to make his ship fly?"

16

PETER

I didn't like the pallor of her skin, nor the bruising under her eyes. I almost missed her question to Tinkerbell as my gaze lingered over her.

But I did hear it.

"How do you think Silver is able to make his ship fly?"

The Henrietta was a formidable pirate ship. She had sailed valiantly through the Caribbean. I knew because I had been there as a young boy. Before all the shit went down with Hook, and we ended up in Neverland.

I had thought at one point when I left Neverland that I would begin to age again. But it seemed that mythical island had claimed me for its own. Wendy, John, and Michael's bodies aged in their natural progression.

But around the age of twenty-five I'd stopped aging.

When Silver and his crew showed up I half expected them to be corpses. But Long John Silver looked the same way he had all those years ago in England.

There were so many questions and not enough answers.

Tinkerbell's eyes narrowed, "You think he has a fairy aboard?"

Ebony shrugged, "I have wondered. What else would produce

enough pixie dust to carry this ship into the sky? Does anyone know where they have been all these years?"

I spoke, "I've tried to get it out of Black Dog, I figured he would break down. But they aren't talking unless it is to insult each other."

"I have firsthand knowledge of that," Ebony smirked and my gut clenched.

Damn, the woman was effortlessly beautiful. And she was the smartest woman I'd ever known.

I wanted to be better, someone that Ebony deserved. That was why I had kept away. I wanted more than a stolen night here or there.

"If I find out," Tinkerbell bargained, "Your wish won't be rescinded?"

Ebony nodded. "Yes, I will keep my wish that you remain human-sized if that is what you want."

Tinkerbell nodded and turned to leave, but before she had taken two steps she turned around and came back.

"I am sorry, if I haven't been as I ought to you, Captain."

Ebony's jaw dropped. "Tinkerbell?"

"I am not used to being treated fairly. I don't know if that is because of my pixie size or because people couldn't hear me talking. But you are one of the first humans that has ever treated me well. I will do my best."

She turned on her heels and walked out, with determination in every step.

Ebony's eyes were wide. "You did hear that, right? I'm not dreaming?"

I smiled. "I am as surprised as you are."

Her brow furrowed, "I hadn't thought about my treatment of her. But I know that I brought her on this voyage. She didn't choose to come, and I didn't ask her. What kind of person does that?"

I couldn't hold in the chuckle. "A pirate, that's what kind."

Her cheeks pinked. "I'm not really a pirate."

I climbed into the berth with Ebony and cradled her in my arms. "Why do you say that?"

"Everything on Neverland…? I had thought it was real. But it's not, is it? Your world was raw and frightening. But I felt alive for the first time. What does it all mean?"

I pressed a finger against her brow. "You are thinking too hard."

Her eyes narrowed. "I'm serious!"

I leaned over and kissed her nose. "I am too. Listen, Ebony, I feel much the same way. I am nervous to return to a land I had half convinced myself didn't even exist. I don't know what the future will hold. But I do know that you need some sleep."

"I'm not tired," she said, pouting until I caught her lower lip in my teeth.

Ebony sank into the kiss. Her hands tangled in my hair and tugged. I felt a jolt go straight to my cock.

It was already half hard just being near her. The taste of her mouth caused my insides to shudder with need.

My hands found their way underneath her layers. I loved how she melted with every touch of my fingertips. Growling low in my throat, I pulled her under me.

We yanked at our clothes, me shoving my pants down and kicking them off as she tossed her thick sweaters onto the floor below.

Her skin no longer felt cold. I could touch her all day; she felt like the finest silk under my fingertips.

Her mouth dropped open and a low moan filled the air as I took one of her nipples and flicked it with my tongue.

Ebony writhed beneath me, teasing every inch of my body.

I flipped our positions so that she could lay atop my chest. She looked at my flat brown nipples and looked at me questioningly. I gasped as her warm mouth covered it. Using her teeth, she gently tugged, and I couldn't hold back the growl that escaped my lips.

Ebony looked up at me, her expression surprised and more than a little pleased.

"You like that?" her husky voice reminded me of whiskey.

"Hell, yeah," I rasped and then steeled myself when she went back to playing. Sucking and flicking until I was gripping her hips and grinding her heat against my swollen dick.

"No more teasing!" I demanded hotly.

Her face was triumphant, and so endearing. I felt my heart crack, and I hadn't realized that I still had one after all these years.

"I like teasing," she grinned, her cheeks flushed with color and her eyes dark with lust.

"I like fucking," I replied and tried to get her to sink down on me.

"Not yet," Ebony raised a brow. "I have more exploring to do."

She slid further down my legs and took my cock into her hands.

"Shit!" I hissed as she stoked the length. "Ebony, that feels so good."

Her eyes brightened, and she increased her speed. I wrapped my hand around hers to show her what I liked. Where to squeeze and hold for maximum pleasure.

Then to my complete shock she leaned down and licked the silvery pre-cum that had appeared at the tip.

My patience level was gone.

"Fuck!"

She must have heard the raw plea in my voice, because she climbed back up and positioned my dick at her entrance.

I couldn't wait any longer. Shoving my hips forward I impaled myself into her heat. Ebony cried out as I rammed my cock hard and fast into her lithe body. I had her breasts in my hands, molding them and teasing their peaks.

"I am going to fuck these one day," I growled, and her eyes grew wide.

"How does that work?" she panted, grinding her wet pussy down hard.

"Another day," I rasped. "Turn around."

She stopped, tilting her head to the side. "What?"

"Turn around, Ebony, bend over and grab my thighs for support."

She did as I asked her and her slender back and perfect ass became my view. There wasn't an inch of her that I didn't adore.

Sinking back onto my dick she moaned low in her throat, "You are so deep."

I grabbed her ass cheeks and pressed down as I lifted my hips, "Ride me, Ebony. Make yourself cum."

She began to rock, my cock slipping deeper and deeper inside of her. The mewls of desire escaped her lips until I felt her begin to tense.

I increased my speed, meeting her thrust for thrust. She was so fucking sexy; I was having a hard time holding on to my release. Suddenly, it was ripped from me as she shattered, coating my dick and balls with her juice.

I had just come inside of her; no condom, no pulling out.

I wasn't worried that there might be a baby. I have always wanted to be a father. But I didn't want to take that choice from her.

She turned around, saying sheepishly. "I can't believe I just did that. All you could see was my ass! How humiliating!"

I pulled her tight against me. "Your ass is incredible. I could look at it all day."

She shook her head against my neck. "You are the crazy one!"

She was right, I was crazy about her.

17

EBONY

"Ebony! I need to talk to you!" Tinkerbell came flying up to the deck at breakneck speed.

I had been speaking with Captain Silver. I refused to call him my father, because he was very much still a stranger to me. I was not opposed to getting to know him better, though.

What had I learned? Well, Captain Long John Silver was rather easy to talk to. He liked almost everyone and often had a smile on his face. His crew didn't fear him, but there was a deep-seated respect.

He was a very different Captain than Hook had been. Much more like myself, and I didn't want to delve further into that thought.

"Ebony," Tink was now tugging on my arm. "This is urgent!"

Captain Silver grinned. "It would appear that your fairy needs your assistance."

I turned to Tinkerbell. "What is it?"

Her mouth tightened. "In private!"

"Oh!" I turned to Captain Silver who was looking on in amusement. "Please excuse me, I am needed elsewhere."

He merrily waved a hand as if to say that all was well with the world. I didn't have much time to think about it, as Tink was dragging me to the other end of the ship.

"For goodness sake, Tink! Whatever is the matter with you?" I wrenched my arm away from her and rubbed the spot that now tingled from her tight grasp.

"I found out how they make the ship fly!"

I clapped a hand over her mouth and hissed in her ear, "Are you serious?"

Her bright blue eyes twinkled, and she nodded.

"We can't discuss this here," I breathed quietly. "Meet me in my cabin in ten minutes. I will round up Peter."

Tinkerbell nodded and scurried off. I looked up to the rigging to where Peter was helping to repair a sail.

His already fit body was starting to show the effects from the constant physical demands of sailing. Peter's shoulders seemed a mite broader and his legs more muscular. I felt a frisson of heat between my thighs.

True to his word, he had stayed with me every night since he found me in the hammock. It was intoxicating just lying near him, but the things he did to my body had me coming undone at the seams.

"Ebony!" he shouted, "Is everything alright?"

Damn, he had to have seen me staring like a love-sick fool. Flushing wildly, I motioned for him to climb down.

Peter swung on the ropes like a professional acrobat. Never once hesitating, he treated the rigging as if it were a playland and not the death trap that it could be. Not only were there myriad ropes but long cross beams had often caused a sailor to trip and fall. It was frightening in the ocean, but in space there would be no way to rescue someone who fell.

My heart in my throat, I watched him, praying every moment until his feet hit the deck.

He took my shoulders in his hands and I felt the warmth from him infuse my body.

"What is the matter?" Peter always came right to the point. I liked that about him.

"Come with me," I turned, and made my way below deck, to our small cabin.

Peter raised a brow but didn't comment as he followed my lead.

Once we had entered the cabin he gathered me close and kissed my forehead almost as if he couldn't keep his hands or lips from finding some part of my body.

I felt an immediate response, but it was quelled by the other person waiting in the room.

"I will throw-up," Tink made gagging noises from the small chair that was bolted down in the corner.

"Why are you here?" Peter demanded, trying to push me behind him.

"I asked her to come!" I quickly intervened, before they started to squabble. Apparently, there was a lot of animosity lingering between the two after Tink had treated Wendy so badly all those years ago in Neverland.

I tried not to be jealous - emphasis on trying. What point was there to being jealous of a dead woman? I wasn't going to think about that either.

"Tink," I turned what I hoped to be a charming smile on the fairy. "What did you find out about how they were keeping the ship aloft?"

Her gaze sharpened. "Oh, Ebony, you aren't going to like this."

I felt a sneaking suspicion in my gut that she was right.

"Just tell us," Peter demanded gruffly.

Tinkerbell huffed, "I was trying to, before you interrupted!"

Laying a quelling hand on Peter's arm I encouraged, "What did you find out, Tink?"

"He has the devil's sprite working for him. The Welsh call him Pwca. I've heard others refer to him as the Hobgoblin. He is a trickster, and the worst sort of fairy imaginable. His true name is Robin Goodfellow, but to everyone else he goes by…"

"Puck."

Peter and Tink said his name at the same time. It sounded almost like a curse.

"How did they find Puck?" Peter was livid.

"I don't know?" Tink was wringing her hands together. "Ebony, you don't understand how awful Puck can be. I am in fear for us all. He has much greater skill with magic than I do, and he is known for his terrible tricks."

"Where are they keeping him?" Peter demanded. "I can't believe that Robin Goodfellow would allow himself to be caged."

"He's not caged," Tink refuted. "He is in human-size form much like myself. You have seen him on deck, I am certain of it. I just thought he was a rather handsome pirate. I hadn't a clue that he was Puck. His glamor must be iron-clad."

"What name is he going by?" I asked, "How will we know it is Puck?"

Tink swallowed. "I will point him out to you. He is tall, broad chested and narrow waisted."

Peter scowled. "You just described more than half the men onboard."

Tink fluttered nervously, and her cheeks heated. "Oh! Shut-up Peter!"

I gave him a quelling look that conveyed that he wasn't helping.

"Tink, I will come up with you to the deck. Do you think you could point him out without Puck noticing?"

Tink straightened. "Of course, I can."

She hopped up and went straight to the door. Peter and I followed her up to the deck looking a little like goslings following their mother.

Her eyes swept around the deck, but she didn't seem to find who she was looking for.

Peter rolled his eyes and went back to the rigging. "We will talk more about this later."

I nodded and turned back to Tink.

She sighed, "Perhaps he is off duty?"

I hadn't seen anyone off duty unless they were sleeping, but I didn't bring up that point to Tink. With a frustrated smile I patted her hand and turned to leave. I was thankful for the information that she had found out. Tink was indeed invaluable on our trip.

"Thank you, Tink," I said softly. I wanted her to know that I truly was grateful.

But before I could expound further, a large man came up the stairs. His mischievous eyes searched the space before alighting on Tinkerbell.

I would swear later that the violet color deepened as a smirk spread across his rugged chin. He had longish back hair tied back in a que. He was dressed much like the other pirates, but he was undeniably handsome.

He strode over to us with a determined air. I held my breath, not knowing what the King of Tricksters might do to us. But when he bowed and took Tinkerbell's hand into his large one I wasn't the only person to drop their jaw in astonishment.

"Tinkerbell," his voice coated us like dark chocolate. "It has been far too long."

Tinkerbell tried to tug her hand back, but Puck held it as if it were nothing.

Turning to me, she gave me a look of pure terror.

Fuck, and I'd been starting to hope that things were looking up.

18

PETER

"Release her!" I hadn't even realized I had spoken until Puck turned to smirk at me.

"Ah! Jim Hawkins, how did I know that you would somehow get yourself entangled in this mess?"

"Let Tinkerbell go," I said through gritted teeth. I hated this man/fairy/prick with everything that was in me.

Puck was as old as time. And when I first met Tinkerbell she was under his control, much like a slave would be. I knew Tinkerbell could be a pain in the ass, but no one deserved to be chained to Robin Goodfellow.

Puck raised a brow. "No."

"Oh, for the love of Triton, let the fairy go!" Silver boomed, and Puck immediately released her hands.

This was interesting. Puck usually only answered to Oberon, the king of the fairies. For Silver's word to incite the same type of obedience was curious indeed.

Puck scowled. "I wasn't harming the ladybird."

Ebony's brows rose.

There have been many definitions of the term 'ladybird' over the years. In truth it is a small beetle with a domed back, usually red or yellow with black spots. In recent years it could be meant as complimentary, as in someone who looks just as good coming as they do going.

But I had a feeling Puck meant neither of those definitions. Because a hundred years ago or so the term 'ladybird' referred to one's mistress or even a prostitute. It was not for a lady, but for a woman of ill-repute.

Now, I am not one to judge, and I know that Tink has had more paramour's than eyelashes in her lifetime. But a man didn't sit back and watch a woman be insulted.

I pulled the sword from its sheath and advanced.

Ebony screamed, but Black Dog caught her before she could intervene. Captain Silver seemed to be yelling something and Tink was harshly shoved to the side as Puck brandished a sword of his own.

"It's nice to see that you are still in there, Peter Gallagher," Puck taunted.

"You will apologize to the lady, Puck," my voice was deceptively quiet, and laced with malice.

"You may have beaten me all of those years ago, Peter," he spat my name. "But times have changed, and I am not the same boy you bested all those years ago. Besides, I don't see a lady present."

"What is he talking about?" Ebony cried out, but I ignored her. For me to take my eyes off Puck for even a second would be folly. He had now included Ebony in his insult.

"Tell me, Peter," Puck taunted, "How have you liked your banishment from fairyland?"

I swore beneath my breath, "You will apologize, you guttersnipe!"

But Puck's face had turned at Ebony's surprised cry.

"What is this? Do they not know who Peter Gallagher truly is? This is indeed a grand surprise!"

"What are you talking about?" Ebony stared him down, like a queen. "He is Peter Pan."

"A name he took up as a youth when his days of rabble rousing with me ended," Puck sneered, and Tink hung her head. "You see, our dear Peter Gallagher was once a celebrated member of the fairy guild. But he betrayed his own and was cast off forever."

Tink lifted her head. Her eyes were full of shame and sorrow.

"Peter never betrayed anyone. He rescued me from this monster. In fairyland a tinker is little more than a slave. When it was discovered, Peter was banished to earth. That was when he got tangled up with the pirates."

Captain Long John Silver came forward. His wooden leg clanked against the deck as he meandered forward, disregarding the two men with swords at each other's throats.

"I had wondered where you came from," Silver stroked his white beard, "It makes sense that you are more than a mere mortal, and why you should have changed your name to hide who you had been."

That had been a long time ago and I had no wish to rehash the past.

"Where did Tinkerbell go?" Ebony asked quietly. "When you came to earth for your banishment? What happened to her?"

Puck laughed, "The naughty sprite has never been loyal. She didn't want to leave fairyland, and so she went into hiding. It was then she was cursed to remain tiny and at the whim of a human's wish."

I had the feeling that Tink was going to do something stupid, so I acted quickly. I brought my sword down and it clanked loudly as it struck Puck's. His eyes narrowed, and, in an instant, the cold-blooded predator came out in him.

He met my sword thrust for thrust, advancing, and then retreating in the age-old dance of fencing. His skills were much improved from the last time our steel had met. But I was still better.

Arm moving with precision, my sword flew in a flurry of angles and arches. Puck lunged in attack. I parried his opening blow and nearly snagged his shoulder with my riposte. Soon we were brandishing our swords at so rapid a rate that one couldn't tell where the clanking of metal was coming from. Sweat began to bead on his brow and I smiled knowing that it would only irritate Puck further.

"You always were a pompous ass, Peter!" he snarled at me, and I used his jab to make one of my own. But I used my sword, slicing the top of his arm.

I didn't cut him deeply, but you would have thought that I'd severed it by his thunderous expression.

Puck began to fight wildly, showing signs of exhaustion and making mistakes. I nicked him again on the thigh and he grazed my chest.

I hardly noticed the sting, but I didn't miss Ebony's horrified, indrawn breath.

I needed to end this as quickly as possible. The last thing I wanted to do was frighten her. I shouldn't have let the old devil rile me. The hiss of the blade came rather close to my ear but with a flick of my wrist I was able to draw him in close and smack his wrist hard enough with the hilt of my sword to make him drop his.

"Are you man enough to finish this off?" Puck spat at me, not caring about the sweat that coursed down both of our faces.

"I have no wish to kill you, Puck. Or I would have done so eons ago, you know that you've given me enough provocation through the years."

I bowed and released him.

"But you will apologize to the ladies, if you please."

Puck knew he had been bested. So, in an instant he went from swordsman to allowing a brilliant smile crossed his lips and he bowed as if addressing royalty.

"My dear, *ladies,* please do not take offense from me. I am truly sorry if I harmed your delicate sensibilities in any way."

Fucking prick.

Tink eyed him warily, but Ebony choked out a laugh. "Do you have a standard apology that you use? Or was that for our effect only? I must admit, very impressive."

She couldn't have done anything to feed his ego more. Puck felt that his acting skills were superb and second to none.

He faked a blush. "My dear, I haven't the foggiest idea what you are speaking about. But I declare, "You are the most beautiful creature I have ever laid eyes on."

"Is he for real?" Ebony turned to me and pointed a thumb back toward my childhood friend turned nemesis.

Puck beamed. "I guarantee you, fair lady, that I am one hundred percent masculine perfection beneath these rags. If you have a wish to verify that?"

My sword was immediately at his throat again.

His lips twitched. "So, that is how the wind blows?"

I moved forward so the tip pricked his skin. "You will not come near Ebony, or I assure you today will be your last."

19

EBONY

Neverland had been sighted, and the ships sailed their plotted course, rushing ever closer to Hook. The arrival loomed over me in a way that defied description. I had never been so nervous about going home. But the kicker was that it really wasn't home, not anymore.

It wasn't like Hook was the kindest of fathers. I don't have memories of parental chats or bedtime stories. But he had been mine for quite some time, every horrible inch of him. To learn that it was all a lie, well, I felt numb.

Puck had been restrained by Silver for the remainder of the voyage. I haven't the foggiest notion how it was accomplished. I had enjoyed getting to know Silver in the few short weeks that we had spent onboard.

But I had a sneaking suspicion that I didn't know him any better than I had that first night they commandeered the Jolly Roger. For, as congenial and witty as the man was, Silver was also crafty and sly.

Peter had been distant as well. I knew that he was shaken up by Puck's appearance on the scene. It was boggling to think that Peter was once one of the fae. I didn't ask him if he had any of the magic still within him. But I figured that it had to be there somewhere.

What would a fairy want with a human?

The thought plagued me. And was I truly human or something else? There were too many conflicting thoughts and emotions swirling about. I half expected Hook to advance on us as we entered Neverland's atmosphere. But there was nothing, not even an ounce of trouble.

We landed to the east, just past Skull Rock. As the ships reunited with the sea there was a mighty groan from the timber. We still needed to sail north past Hangman's Tree to the Indian Camp where Princess Tiger Lily would be returned to her people.

It would be then that the Lost Boys could return to their homes and, finally, we would go in search of Hook.

"What are you doing over here all alone?" I glanced up to see Tink wearing a curious expression.

I looked out at the sea and smelled the familiar, salty air, "Did you miss it? While we were gone?"

"Neverland?" she asked, surprised.

I nodded. "I know that it isn't your first home, but you have become an integral part of Neverland over the years."

Tink smiled softly. "In my first home I was a slave. I worked from dusk till dawn and was treated like an animal. I do not miss fairyland, nor its people. Neverland accepted me as one of their own. I was celebrated. No one could do what I can with a flip of my wrist or a nod of my head. Even with the punishment of being subject to human's wishes, I am free. I know that I haven't always been the friendliest, Ebony. I have a hard time trusting, and now that you know my past—you see why."

I turned to the curvy blonde woman. "I understand much more than you think. I hope that you have reason to begin to trust me."

She bit her lip. "You have been fair with me Captain, and I will show you the same loyalty. With that said, I feel that I must warn you. Something is amiss in Neverland. I feel it against my skin like a whispered plea."

I looked back out over the water to the cliffs. We weren't far from the Indian Camp.

"I too feel that eerie sense of foreboding."

It was at that moment that arrows began to rain upon us from the land. There was a cry as a pirate was hit in the rigging and fell to his death in the water below.

I grabbed Tink's arm and dropped like a stone to the deck. There was screaming of orders from Silver and men's cries as they loaded the cannons for battle. I wondered what Princess Tiger Lily could be thinking. These were her people. If any were killed it would be like losing a part of herself.

I hadn't seen Alex or Lily as they sailed the Jolly Roger. I wondered if they had resolved their differences- or if they were still dancing around each other in a painful but strangely intriguing minuet.

"Stop!" I heard her scream from the other deck and knew that they had sailed in close to us. "Don't kill them!"

But Silver paid her no heed and ordered the first round of shots to be fired.

There was chaos as Tinkerbell and I tried to get closer to the action. With the enemy on land and us on the sea, it made sense to sail further out until we could assess the situation.

I had made my way from the back deck to the ship's wheel where I instructed the sailor who was manning it to step down. He blinked once and swallowed twice, but wasn't about to contradict Captain Ebony Hook, natural daughter of Captain Long John Silver.

Silver soon figured out my plot and was racing as quickly as his peg leg would allow to my location.

"What is the meaning of this? I am the Captain!"

I stared him down. "You are not from Neverland."

"Why in the bloody hell should that matter?" he growled, trying to take the wheel from my hands.

"We need a plan," I shouted. "We don't kill first and figure it all out later."

"That's always worked for me." He yanked the wheel, and I almost lost my grip.

"Well," I yanked back as hard as I could, "maybe, you could listen to someone else once in a while?"

"Damn it, girl! That is a terrible idea if I ever heard one!" he challenged. I could see sweat forming on his brow.

I too was sweaty and tired, but not beaten.

"If you truly want me to ever consider you as my father…," I began.

He jerked back, his hands almost leaving the wheel. "I am your father!"

I went on as if he hadn't spoken, "If you want me to think of you as my father you need to start treating me like your daughter! I have knowledge of this land and these people. Before you go in guns blazing and ruin this entire world, let's make a plan!"

His grimy teeth were gritted, and his knuckles showed white where he was holding the wheel so that I couldn't steer us away. But his eyes were locked on mine, and I knew he was considering my words.

"Captain!"

We both turned to the crewman that had called out.

It was Black Dog. "We have lost seven men, sir! What are your orders?"

Silver looked back at me, and for a moment I feared that he would demand Black Dog remove me from the deck. But he didn't.

After a pregnant pause, he shouted, "Fall back! Do you hear, fall back!"

He released the wheel, and I nearly went sprawling to the deck in surprise as the momentum shook my arms. Then Silver began helping me turn the ship. It was arduous work. But we labored in tandem until we were out of range from the camp.

The Jolly Roger followed the Henrietta and a short while later Tiger Lily and Alex sailed across on the ropes.

She went straight to Silver. "I don't know how she did it. But thank you."

Silver blushed. His voice was gruff, as he dithered, "I didn't need any encouragement, Princess."

Alex raised a brow, "We saw you and Ebony having quite a *discussion*."

Silver growled.

"My father," I swallowed as all eyes turned to me. Taking a shaky breath, I continued, "My father saw the wisdom in retreating for the moment so that we could rejoin efforts and win the battle."

I thought for a split second that Silver might cry. His lip trembled, and he cleared his throat, "It is as my daughter said. I don't want to go in *guns blazing* until we know what we are up against."

Lily went up to Silver and shocked him to the core by kissing his whiskered cheek.

"I won't forget this, Silver," she vowed.

I wasn't sure the man could take this much affection and goodwill on the same day.

Silver turned to the crew which was standing at attention, awaiting orders.

"Pan! Puck! Tinkerbell! We met immediately in my cabin. There is much to discuss." He turned to Charlie, "You will be in charge in my absence."

Nate and Tom scowled at this, but Charlie beamed. "Aye, aye, Captain!"

And a pirate was born.

20

PETER

I am not one for drinking. Having lived as long as I have, one finds that shitty hangovers aren't fun. And besides, everyone knows that human alcohol tastes like swill.

Perhaps that is why I caved in to temptation, when the Trickster King pulled out an aged bottle of mulled fairy rum. Or it very well could have been the fact that I had fallen hopelessly and madly in love with Ebony.

I felt a tremendous amount of guilt for not being honest with her about my origins. But that part of my life seemed to be a millennium ago. As far as I knew, the fairy council didn't recognize my existence.

I hadn't seen my family in so long it was almost as if they'd never existed.

When Puck showed up with a fairy drink and news from my brother, I caved.

The rum felt like syrup coating my teeth and tongue before rolling lazily down my throat.

Pure bliss.

"Damn!" I said appreciatively, "Where did you find this?"

Puck leaned back against the ropes. We were perched in the

crow's nest. On the morrow, we were to infiltrate the island and find out what in the hell had happened. It had been Ebony's idea.

Ebony.

Her long brown hair and flashing eyes caused my chest to ache with want and need. I would talk to her. I had too.

But first, I wanted to know about my brother.

"Obviously, I swiped it from the fairy court," he boasted, as a faint smile crossed his face. "I may not have been the fastest at retrieving the goods, but I still have my ways."

I huffed, remembering years gone by. "Sticky fingers, that's what Jim would call me when I appropriated something without the owner's permission. I was so proud of the moniker. Lord knows that it's a terrible thing to be known for."

Puck shrugged. "We were kids. Isn't that a rite of passage or something?"

I nodded, taking another sip of the rich rum.

"I suppose," my eyes met his. "Is that your excuse for all the havoc you have caused?"

Puck grinned, and I saw in that smile the friend of my childhood.

"Robin Goodfellow was a right twit," Puck chuckled. "I sometimes wonder if I will ever outlive my actions back then."

I felt myself slipping into a nice buzz. It loosened my tongue when I usually would have kept my peace.

"Why are you here, Puck?"

He looked at me for a long moment. "You wouldn't believe me if I told you."

I considered his answer because it was most likely true. But with a bit of wine in my belly, I was feeling generous.

"Nonsense, you were my sworn blood brother, have you forgotten?"

The corner of Puck's mouth twitched. "How could I forget? You almost severed my hand making the oath."

I had the decency to appear shamefaced but then ruined it by laughing.

He tossed a bit of straw at my head. I've no idea where that came from. And then he offered to refill my glass that was surprisingly empty.

With another cup of fortification, I asked again, "Why are you here, Puck?"

"I am not the same boy that I once was," he began. "How do you live down centuries of mistakes and misdeeds?"

I raised a brow. "Going on the straight and narrow?"

I knew my question sounded incredulous. It was only that Puck was the Trickster King.

He met my gaze. His violet eyes were solemn as he said, "Silver made some type of bargain with Oberon, and God help him if he doesn't complete his end of it. I wasn't supposed to be the fairy assigned to this voyage. Your brother Jim had volunteered in exchange for the council reconsidering your status."

I was speechless.

Puck nodded, "Jim has been petitioning the court for over a hundred years now."

"Why would they even consider it?" my tone was harsh, as I tried to process what I was hearing. "I was judged and convicted. They wouldn't go against their *favorite,* Goodfellow."

Puck sighed and rubbed the back of his neck. "Yeah, well, I petitioned with Jim and told the council the truth about my treatment of Tink."

I looked at my cup which was rapidly losing rum to my belly.

"Why would you do that?"

Puck leaned forward. "I was in love with Tink. But I was only a child and hadn't the capacity to know how to treat her. I didn't have parents as a guide, only the royal court who treats everyone like shit and smiles about it. Look, Peter, I was wrong. I ruined your life, hers, and probably a million others. I am not proud of it."

I shook my head and felt it sloshing about. It was time to put down the drink.

"Why now?" I demanded, "Why after all of these years are you trying to do the right thing?"

There was sorrow in those violet depths, "You and Tink deserve to come home."

"And the council hopped on board with that?" I spat, knowing that those bastards would do nothing of the sort.

"No," he said simply. "I got myself banished along with you."

"Fuck," I breathed, "What a stupid ass thing to do!"

A ghost of a smile crossed his lips. "You have changed, Peter. For the better, but it is strange for me to reconcile the man with the boy I knew. Anyhow, Jim was to accompany Silver. So, I tied him up and took his place. By the time he got free, I had already sailed with Silver."

"And that is why the good Captain has you by the balls," I figured, putting the pieces together. "He knew that you weren't supposed to be the one."

Puck nodded. "But because of my history with you, he allowed it on the condition that I don't have any screw ups. The swordplay on the deck notwithstanding, I have been rather well behaved."

I scoffed, "You always did have a hot temper."

Puck laughed, "Pot? Might you have a moment to greet your equal, Kettle?"

I saluted him. "Just so, my friend, just so."

He paused, staring.

"What?" I looked about me.

Puck swallowed. "Nothing, it is only that it's been a long time since you have claimed me as your friend."

I frowned. "It is most likely the drink talking."

He nodded. "Most likely."

"I shall probably want to run you through when I am sober," I continued.

"Most definitely," he agreed. But there was hope in his eyes that hadn't been there before.

I smiled at him. "People can change, Puck."

He gave a shuddering sigh. "God help me, I hope so. About that message from your brother?"

I felt a knot in my throat. The last thing my brother had said to me was that he was ashamed that we shared the same blood and that I was never to call upon him, because Peter Gallagher was dead.

"Yes," I was barely able to squeeze out the word.

"Jim wanted to tell you himself," Puck was looking into the distance, his voice low, "but he had talked with me enough about it that I feel I can get the main idea across. Jim knew that you took his name when you were first banished. It almost ruined him that you still idolized him after he had so ruthlessly cut you off. We became friends over the years, and Jim long since wished that he had never said the things that he did."

I felt something wet in my lashes and swiped at my eyes harshly, "Damn sea winds!"

"I really am sorry, Peter," Puck hung his head. "For all of it."

I kicked his boot until he looked at me. "I don't give a flying fuck about who you were, Puck. That is over and done with. But you are going to need to prove yourself, not only with me but with everyone."

He nodded. "That's all I ask."

21

EBONY

I had crawled into my bunk only to sit and stare at the wall. I hated the room without Peter. But I was not about to go crawling to him. A woman had her pride, or at least what was left of it after this hellacious trip.

I heard muffled singing, something about a pirate life or something. I leaned up on my elbow to try and hear more clearly when the door burst open and Peter came stumbling in with the help of Puck.

"Get away from him!" I shouted, jumping off the bed and racing to Peter's side.

Puck's handsome face broke into a knowing grin, "I am just returning him to you. And for the record, if I hadn't he would have broken his neck trying to walk off the crow's nest."

"Walk off? What in the world are you talking about?"

But Puck didn't have time to answer because Peter had caught sight of me and was slipping his hands inside of my pants.

"Peter, fuck!" I squealed as his fingers brushed my ass.

"Yeah," his voice was low and thick, "I want to fuck. That is a fantastic idea."

He picked me up and nearly had us falling to the floor.

"What did you do to him?" I demanded of Puck, who was trying not to laugh his ass off.

"I did nothing," Puck said innocently. "He may have had a glass or two too many by the looks of things."

"What was he drinking?" I cried out as Peter started to grind his long cock against me right on the floor.

"Rum," Puck backed away, amusement apparent as Peter sucked loudly on my neck.

"Ouch! Why is he like this?"

"Fairy drink can make one amorous, and with that, I bid you both a good night."

"Night, Robin!" Peter grinned at Puck who was closing the door, "Bloody good fellow Puck, it's like his name, Goodfellow!"

Peter laughed at his drunken wittiness and Puck closed the door with a sharp tug.

"He's my friend. Did you know that Ebony? I know he was bad, but he's going to be good now, and Jim doesn't hate me."

"What in the fuck are you talking about?" I was so lost! "How did Puck convince you to give him another chance? He kept Tinkerbell as a slave, Peter!"

Peter blinked as if trying to clear his mind. "He's sorry. Sometimes when you are bad, you say sorry, Eb. I know you don't like to be wrong. But it does happen. I am wrong all the time."

"I don't like to be wrong?" I said dangerously.

He nodded happily. "Like right now. You are likely going to hit me, and then you will have to say sorry. That's how it works."

You must be fucking kidding me.

"I will show you," He leaned in and kissed my lips.

Nibbling against the tender flesh, he licked the seam until I relented, and he swept inside. My pussy clenched with need and my heart nearly leaped from my chest. But we had things to resolve.

I shoved against his chest until he begrudgingly moved back.

"Peter," I was hot and getting wet, but still confused and angry enough to not jump into bed. "You have been walking around here like a bear with a sore head ever since we discovered Puck. Now, you act as though you are best friends. I need to know what is going on."

Peter placed me on my feet and stood up next to me with only a little wobble. He yanked his clothes off, despite my squawking protests, and then began to remove mine.

"Eb, the thing was that I was wrong." He almost sounded lucid. "But I didn't want to say sorry to you."

"That's a horrible thing to say!" I bristled and tugged my shirt back over my breasts.

He raised a brow. "Now you are being mean."

"Why didn't you want to say sorry to me?" I huffed.

A light pink tinged his cheeks. "Because I was afraid you wouldn't want to be with me. Don't tell anyone, but I am really a fairy."

The humor of this large muscular man telling me that he was a fairy was not lost on me.

My lips twitched. "I am aware of that fact."

His brow rose. "You are?"

Peter had practically shouted it.

"Do you still want to be with me, Ebony? Because in the spirit of honesty I feel that I need to tell you that I am in love with you. I want to have babies with you. Erm, maybe you will carry the babies, I don't have a uterus."

He had literally lost his mind.

"Why?" I felt a flare of hope in my chest, but I needed to know if this was real and not just good fairy rum. "Why do you love me?"

His green eyes darkened, and he cupped my face in his large hands.

"I love the way you glance down at the floor and bite your lip when you are nervous. I love the way you take whatever comes your way in stride. I love the way you have opened yourself up to a relationship with your father, despite how hard I know it must be. I love that you have been so kind to Tink, even though I know what a pill she can be. I love the way you face danger with a level head and a cool blade. But mostly, I love the look in your eyes when you watch me and don't know that I can see you. You like me, Ebony."

I tried to swallow the giant knot in my throat.

"How do I look at you?" I choked out, knowing damn well what he was talking about.

"Like I am a king or a god. I can't let that light go out of your eyes."

"And you believe that if I knew you were a fairy and not just a man that would change things?" I cupped his jaw. "I love you, too, Peter."

He shook his head, "You can't love me. No one loves me."

"How can you say that? Peter, I am sure that there have been people who have loved you."

"Wendy loved me like a brother, but she wasn't in Neverland long enough to become immortal. She and her brothers grew up and were gone." He sighed, "I don't want to talk about this."

I leaned up to pull his face down to rest his forehead on mine, "I love you. I don't care if you are Jim Hawkins, or Peter Pan, or Peter Gallagher. I love the man you are, not a name or a species."

He smiled, and my heart melted into a puddle of goo. "I think I might be a little drunk. You just said that you love me."

He swept me up in his arms and carried me over to the berth then, laying us down upon the coverlet.

I giggled at Peter's scowling expression. Obviously, he wanted the shirt off. In one smooth movement, he had it up and over my head.

I ran a finger over the front of his boxer briefs where his dick was straining against the fabric. I was completely naked and wanted him to be the same.

But I was curious about this part of him.

I pushed Peter onto his back and pulled the elastic away to see his thick, throbbing cock trying to break free. Peter moaned low in his throat when I blew air across the moistened tip.

I nudged him to pick up his hips and slid his underwear down his thighs making his dick spring free. It was slick as silk and thick enough for me to worry that this wouldn't work.

But I wanted to try. I cupped his heavy balls in one hand and he growled out his approval. Then with my other hand I grasped his massive shaft and licked his slit and tasted a man for the first time. He tasted a little salty, musky, and smelled of sensuous heat. I placed the head between my lips, licking the rim before gently pulling him into the hot recesses of my mouth.

"Fuck!" he cried out, trying to clutch the sheets around him.

I smiled with his dick in my mouth. Taking him a bit further, I began to suck and rock my head back and forth. Peter writhed beneath me. I could feel the control he was fighting to hold as my mouth took him deeper and sucked him harder.

The more his toes curled the wetter I became, until my pussy was throbbing with need, and I was sucking him to the back of my throat.

Peter's hands sank into my hair, and he pulled as his body arched off the bed coverings.

"Fuck, Ebony, I am going to cum!"

I knew I could pull off, but I wanted to taste him. I wanted my first time to be a memory that neither of us would ever forget.

I gave his balls a tender squeeze and sucked him as deep as I could do. He cursed loudly, coming hard and fast into my mouth until I couldn't hold it all and some leaked out the side.

Peter was panting. His hands still tangled in my hair as he raised me and watched me lick the remnants of his seed from my lips.

"I do love you," I whispered.

Peter's eyes turned predatory, and I watched as his dick began to grow once more.

"How is that possible?" I gasped.

"There are many benefits to fairy drink," Peter rasped against my lips. "I hope you don't plan on going to sleep tonight."

And why would I? We were just invading the island tomorrow.

But I couldn't have given a shit because Peter loved me, and I bloody well loved every inch of him in return.

22

PETER

I should have known better than to drink so much rum. It had been a long time since I had partaken of fairy food or drink, so it wasn't shocking that I reacted like an untried youth.

The fae have an almost cruel sense of humor. I have often thought that it comes from living too long. The senses become dull, and the fae feel that they must do more, bite harder, and fight longer for any of it to have any meaning.

This is also true in their lovemaking. The fae are and always have been notoriously savage in their fucking. It is usually balls to the wall, hair pulling, and often marks were left behind to show for it.

When Ebony's lips had wrapped around my dick, I knew I was in trouble. I hadn't allowed such liberties with a woman in a long time. Sure, I fucked women here or there, but this was off the table. It brought a certain level of intimacy that left one vulnerable.

With vulnerability comes abandonment, and the last thing I would ever want to do is hurt a woman. It was safer that I stayed away from that practice, until now, until her. Not only had Ebony sucked me off like a champion, but I hadn't fucked her face raw - amazing considering the length of time it had been since I'd had a blowjob and the fairy drink. I knew that this was different, she was the one for me. I couldn't have stopped what happened next if I'd wanted to. And the good Lord knew, I had waited several lifetimes for my one true love.

I wasn't about to let her slide between my fingers.

My lips tasted my release on her tongue, and it only made me hotter. My fingers dug into her shapely hips as I sat up and she straddled my body.

I could smell her arousal mixed with sex and need. It was every bit as heady and intoxicating as the drink had been.

Her large breasts brushed against my chest, and I felt the hardened peaks lightly scrape my skin. Ebony was perfect. From her messy chestnut hair that fell in bedroom waves to the middle of her back and down to her tiny toes that were slightly crooked and overlapped a little.

She had a mole on the side of her mouth that I licked before plundering her depths again. There was something so decadent about making love to someone you loved. Everything felt new again. I felt alive.

Tiny gasps of pleasure escaped her bowed lips as I made my way down her neck with my tongue and teeth. My other hand slipped inside her heat and smiled when I felt just how wet she was for me.

Her pussy was throbbing, aching, and those mewling noises turned into raw groans as my fingers plundered her depths. Her core ached and sucked on my fingertips as I fucked her ever so softly, but deep enough for her to arch her back and thrust those perfect breasts towards my mouth.

I could be a gentleman, but with Ebony, I preferred being the pirate. I latched onto one of her nipples and began to suck, my fingers plunging deeper as I added a third to the mix.

"Fuck, Peter, that feels so amazing!" her hips were writhing in my lap as she rode my hand with abandon.

I bit her nipple gently and was rewarded with a gush of sweet nectar from her pussy. My hands were making a squelching noise as they pumped in and out of her. I began to nibble the other breast.

All the while rubbing that tight, little clit with my thumb and tapping my fingers high inside her pussy.

She screamed my name, throwing her head back and her nipple popped out of my mouth with a resounding sound. I continued to finger her until she shied away from my hand. Aftershocks still rocking her body.

I picked her up and laid her down on the coverlet and then kissed my way down her glorious frame until I could part those lovely thighs.

"I'm too sensitive!" she tried closing her legs.

But I licked her gently, and with a long moan, her thighs fell back open, sharing every inch of her pink perfection.

I tenderly licked her folds, not touching her clit that was over sensitized from her orgasm. Ebony began to move her hips slowly to the rhythm of my tongue. Effortlessly sexy, I watched her body dance as I sucked her pink pussy into my mouth and began to eat her core.

Her arousal was coating my tongue, and I fucking loved it. I picked up her hips and straightened my tongue, thrusting it inside her. When her moves became more frantic, I knew that she was ready.

Moving my mouth up to her clit, I worried it with the flat of my tongue and then sucked it deep inside my mouth.

Her hands shot to my hair while her thighs closed around my head. Her screams were hoarse as she rode out this next orgasm, fucking my face with abandon. When she could handle no more, I placed her right leg over her left, raising it high.

"What are you doing?" her voice was breathy and her eyes tired but filled with lust.

"I am going to fuck you sideways," the words were more of a growl. "I am going to fuck you so hard, Ebony, that you will never doubt who is your equal. You will never want any other man because my cock will reach places in you that you never imagined. When you see the faint bruises on your hips from my fingers you will know who you belong to."

With that, I rammed my aching cock deep. I saw the surprise and wince before her mouth dropped open, and a guttural cry escaped her lips. Hell, yeah, she was into it.

I couldn't contain myself as I thrust into her deeper and harder with each pass. I was balls deep and I almost felt as though I would die if I couldn't find a way to merge our bodies, our souls, into one.

Ebony's hands reached up, and she raked her nails down my chest, leaving long tracks.

"More," her eyes sparkled, and I could have sworn that I saw a hint of fire in them.

If she wanted more, I was happy to deliver it. I picked up her legs and shoved them over my shoulders. Then with her lying on her back, I picked her up so that only her shoulders remained on the bed.

Pumping my cock long and deep I felt her body clench around me.

"Fuck!" I was holding on by a thread, but I didn't want it to be over yet.

Ebony was panting, clutching at the sheets, while her hair matted her forehead with sweat. I had never seen her more beautiful. Suddenly, I had a vision of her being heavy with a child. Her body rounded beautifully, her mouth smiling, and her eyes filled with love.

My release slammed through me, and I came so hard that I saw black dots in front of my eyes.

Ebony's pussy clenched around me, milking out every drop as she convulsed, my orgasm bringing on her own.

I didn't want to pull out. I never wanted to be separated from her. Not by distance, or family, or because I happened to be fae.

"I love you," I rasped. Her breasts were heaving and her eyes cloudy as she tried to focus on what I was saying.

"I love you, too," Ebony pushed her hair back and reached for a cloth.

I reluctantly got up and grabbed something so that I could clean us up before gathering her close.

"I know it's only been a month, but Ebony, you are mine and I am yours. I don't know where we will live or how this will work. But I want to marry you if you will have me."

She stilled in my arms, and I knew I had surprised her.

Shit.

I'd spoken too soon. I shouldn't have let my emotions run away with me. But I hadn't started feeling emotions this strongly until she came into my club. I had thought things like this were beyond my reach. But Ebony had changed everything.

Here I was, throwing it away because I couldn't keep my mouth shut. I needed to be patient.

"We don't have to talk about it right now," I rushed on. "I don't want you to feel pressured or unsure. I am an idiot for forcing this conversation."

Ebony turned and looked directly into my eyes as she placed a finger on my lips, halting my words. My breath caught, and she lightly traced my lips.

"I am tired, and you have had a lot to drink," she began cautiously.

Fuck.

Fuck.

Fuck.

"Ebony, look," I didn't even know what I was going to say.

She gave me a stern look, and I shut up.

"But Peter, if you still feel this way when the current mess we are in is over. My answer will be," her cheeks flushed, and she looked down for a moment and bit her lip. "I love you, Peter—yes, the answer is yes."

23

TINKERBELL

"Dead men don't bite."

-**Robert Lewis Stevenson, Treasure Island**

Charlie was snoring again, and Nate and Tom were feeling frisky. There are only so many times I can pretend not to hear them having sex.

These lost boys are free with their love. I mean that every bit amongst themselves as well as others. For a while, it had been a kick to be one of their playthings.

Tom kissed much like he fucked, fast and furious. Nate was sweet and gentle. And Charlie, he was passionate and hung like a horse.

But despite their sexual gifts, they didn't care for me any more than they did anyone else.

When I walked in on them fucking each other the first time. Tom grinned and asked me to join him and Nate. Charlie was standing near the two lovers stroking his long cock.

When I demurred, Tom shrugged and turned to Charlie, who jumped right in. It couldn't have been clearer to me, in that moment, that I could have been anyone. They didn't want

Tinkerbell. They needed a wormhole to place their dicks, and they weren't particular where they found it.

I watched as Tom thrust his cock into Nate's tight ass and Charlie got on his knees and took Nate's cock into his mouth. It was arousing, and sad at the same time.

I didn't wait until the grand finale and hadn't slept with any of them since.

Perhaps this journey was to be an awakening for me as well? I had watched Ebony change as she embraced her femininity. When the truth of her parentage came into question, she took it all in stride.

She had been incredibly kind to me. In my life, I had been treated many ways, but kind was not often one of them.

Tinker's are the lowest on the fairy food chain. I don't remember my family, nor do I remember friends.

But I do remember Puck.

Nate moaned long and loud, and I sat up from my hammock.

Tom raised an eyebrow in invitation when I saw them wrapped up together on the berth.

I smiled but shook my head and quietly made my way to the door.

"Are we bothering you?" Nate's voice was worried; he was a gentle soul.

Again, I shook my head. "No, I have a bit of a headache. I think some fresh air will be just the thing. I will return shortly."

Nate and Tom had already gone back to kissing when the door shut.

I noiselessly made my way down the corridor towards the stairs leading to the deck. The closer I got to fresh air the more I knew it had been the right decision. I needed to make some changes.

I didn't like who I had become, and I wasn't sure when that had happened. I suppose I stopped caring about what others thought of me long ago. But there had been a time I had deeply cared.

I stared at the night sky, careful not to get too close to the ship's edge. I had no wish to have an arrow through my heart. Even though Silver had assured us that we were far enough out to sea, I didn't trust it.

If something could go wrong, it would go wrong with me wrapped up tightly along with it.

"Hello, Little Light," his dark voice wrapped around me like a cloak.

I whipped my head around to see Puck leaning against the wall.

"You can't take me," I hated the fear in my voice. "Ebony will stop you!"

His brow wrinkled. "Not Peter?"

I rolled my eyes. "I have long since lost all hope for the men in my life."

Puck's violet eyes gleamed, "You have sworn off men?"

I hated how he tied me in knots. "No, I don't trust men. I have never had one be loyal to me."

He blinked, and I saw something strange. I wasn't certain if it was sorrow or regret, but it wasn't something I had ever seen from the infamous Puck before.

"Why are you here?" I demanded bravely.

"Do you ever think about those days?" his tone was whiskey soaked and threatened to drown me.

"No," I said firmly. But it was a lie.

Did I remember how it was when we were together? Puck was part of the royal court, and I was lower than a servant, a mere slave. How could I not remember? There were times when he had held me so close. There were other times when I would feel the tenderness in his gentle caress of my hand.

"You don't recall the nights my head rested between your silky thighs lapping up your cream? You don't ever think about riding my cock, your breasts bouncing with every thrust?"

I gave him my iciest glare. "It must not have been that memorable."

Puck's eyes narrowed, and I expected him to say something cutting. That was his way.

There were too many times when his sharp wit had left me in

tears. Puck had never lifted a hand to me. But he had made it clear that I was the slave and he the master.

"As you say," he turned his head away, and I caught his devastatingly handsome profile.

"What is that supposed to mean?" I demanded hotly.

Puck's violet eyes met mine. "It was a long time ago, Tinkerbell. Perhaps, I have romanticized the past. I will leave you to your quiet."

He shoved off the wall, barely brushing past me, but my skin felt scorched. My reactions to this man were like a moth to a flame. I couldn't allow him to burn me again, and so I said nothing.

But it didn't stop me from watching his every step.

I made my way back down to the cabin I shared with the boys. They had gone between ships during the voyage, but for this night they chose to be together. I heard the action before opening the door.

One guttural cry I knew had to come from Charlie. He must have awoken and joined the fray.

Suddenly, I was exhausted. I laid my forehead against the wooden door. I had no wish to join them in person or spirit. I just wanted to get some sleep. When was the last time I had been able to rest? The sad thing was, I couldn't remember.

"You can have my berth," that voice again, he consistently dogged my steps.

"I am not sleeping with you," my whisper was laced with daggers.

Puck stepped out of the darkness, "I didn't say I would be in it."

I scoffed, "You are telling me that you will allow me to take your bed? Me, a lowly slave taking the bed of a noble lord of fairy?"

His jaw tightened, and he stepped forward. "You are not a slave, Tinkerbell."

"And we are not in fairy," my words hung between us. "I won't allow you to trick me again."

The muscle on the side of his cheek ticked, but he remained calm.

"Tinkerbell, you are in need of rest. There are dark circles under your eyes. I am only offering you a place to sleep."

"And you climb into my bed when I have drifted off?" I laughed harshly, "I know that game already.

"Did I do this to you?" Puck ran a hand through his hair. "Did I make you into this cynical woman that cannot see a hand of kindness when offered?"

Puck hadn't been unkind, but kind—no. I was a slave, little more than a possession. One didn't care about their possessions and certainly not their slaves.

"Life has made me into who I am," I felt my lips tremble, and I tightened them. I wasn't going to cry. I never cried.

"I give you my word as a member of the royal court that I will not allow anyone to disturb the room you are resting in. No one will enter, and you will have your sleep. Is that agreeable to you?"

I was tempted. My body felt bruised, and at that moment I felt every one of my thousand years.

"You swear?" I blurted out, taking a step forward.

"I swear," was his solemn vow.

Minutes later I found myself wrapped in blankets of the softest silk. These were straight from fairy, and it had been an achingly long time since I had felt their softness and been cradled by their warmth.

But it was nothing compared to the scent of Robin Goodfellow. He was the only man I have ever loved, and the person who had shattered my heart.

Little Light- if he only knew, my light had gone out long ago.

24

TINKERBELL

"I have brought you a surprise, Little Light."

I glanced up to see Puck entering his apartments. I had spent much of the day working on a clock mechanism that was broken and I hadn't located the problem yet. I was irritated, cranky, and lonely—not the best combination.

"I don't like surprises," I huffed, turning my back to him, picking up a wrench.

His laughter coated my frayed nerves. "You love surprises. What have you all wrapped up and turned inside out?"

I showed him the little wooden clock.

His eyes narrowed. "Where did you find that?"

I gave an infinitesimal shrug. "In your things."

"I thought that I forbid you from searching my stuff, Tinkerbell," his eyes held a hint of irritation.

"I needed something to do," my eyes flashed to him. "Why are you keeping me here, Puck? You have no use for a Tinker fairy."

His mouth tightened, and I noted the firmness of his chin. Puck's black hair was swept away from his face and his cheekbones were prominent. There was something dangerously masculine about him.

"You are mine, Tinkerbell," he growled, setting the small bag to the side. "I don't need to answer your questions.

I had forgotten about the gift.

"What is that?" I was resigned to the fact that he wasn't going to tell me why I had been taken as a slave. But I couldn't help but needle him about it from time to time.

As far as masters went, Puck wasn't a terrible one. He brought me things, and I had my run of his apartments. What bothered me was that I couldn't leave. He had forbidden me from talking to anyone else.

The only person I saw besides Puck was his friend Peter, and even he didn't know why Puck was so secretive.

Puck tossed the bag to me and I caught it easily. I opened it to see a thin gold chain with a tiny star attached to it.

"I immediately thought of you," he said gruffly.

I lifted it out and noted the fine workmanship. This wasn't a mere trinket but made of excellent fairy gold.

I lifted my hair and held the necklace out to him. Puck took it from my fingers and gently clasped it around my neck. The metal chain felt warm and I swallowed hard. Here was another instance of Puck acting like he cared.

But did he? How could he when I was a prisoner to him?

My eyes popped open and my hand automatically went up to the chain that still to this day hung around my neck. I felt the ridges of the tiny star beneath the pads of my fingers. I don't know why I held on to this gift. It wasn't the most expensive nor the grandest that Puck had given.

But 'Little Light' had always been his nickname for me. How I had loved him; it was both humiliating and shocking to contemplate.

There was a knock at the door.

"Enter," I called out automatically.

Puck closed the door behind him and walked up to the berth where I was laying.

"Are you, all right?" his eyes held concern. "I heard you cry out earlier."

I flushed, "Only a bad dream, it was nothing."

His eyes followed my hands to the necklace before returning to mine.

"You never had nightmares when you slept beside me," his tone was gruff. "I will sit in this chair so that you can rest."

I shook my head. "You cannot go into battle tomorrow after sleeping in a chair."

Puck's mouth broadened into a smile. "Worried about me, Little Light?"

"Worried that you are going to get my ass killed," I shot back with a little heat.

He chuckled. "I am happy to see that your fire is still burning, Tinkerbell."

He pulled up a straight back chair and tried to settle himself. It looked beyond uncomfortable.

"Stop!" I called out, "Just lay here beside me."

His brows rose.

"But don't touch me!"

They rose even higher. "What if my fingers brush your skin?"

I gave him my fiercest glare. "Then I cut them off."

He stood and removed his coat. "Deal."

After shedding his clothing to his underwear, Puck climbed into the berth and I scooted until I was smashed up against the wall.

"Comfortable?" he asked with amusement.

"Peachy," I replied grumpily.

It was a few moments later that I heard his breathing begin to even out. I sighed and scooted over a smidgeon so that I wasn't so cramped. Our sides were touching, and his heat was sending ribbons of desire to my gut. But I chose to ignore it. I was a strong, independent fairy and I didn't need a man.

It was much later before I slipped back into sleep. I didn't notice when his muscular arm wrapped around my waist and pulled me against his chest. Nor did I notice when his legs entangled with mine.

No, I slept like the dead. My dreams are blissfully quiet and my body in perfect contentment.

It was as light began to break that I felt a hardness against the cheeks of my ass. I smiled sleepily and rubbed myself against it. The cock felt massive and somewhat familiar. I was still halfway in dreamland. But I knew that I was waking the male individual in a pleasurable manner.

I low growl emanated through me and the hand that had been wrapped around my waist fingered the elastic of my panties.

I moaned as the other hand reached up to cup my breast, the thumb rubbing lightly over my nipple.

I am not a girl to wait around. If I want something I will go for it. Taking the man's hand, I slid it into my panties and pushed the thick fingers into my slick heat.

I cried out at the invasion. My pussy wept with need as it was stroked by a master. I opened my legs, throwing the top one back so that my lover could have better access.

He slipped two fingers inside my heat and I bit my arm to hold back the cries.

He fingered me languidly, slowly, and thoughtfully, until I was a mess. Blubbering all sorts of nonsense, I begged him to fuck me, begged for his lips, his cock, and his tongue. He began rubbing small tight circles over my clit. His fingers covered in my juices made it more pleasurable and my hips rose to every call of his hand until he bit down gently on my shoulder and I gushed my pleasure out upon his hands.

"Puck!" I cried out, and then stilled. I was no longer asleep, and I was registering that I wasn't in my bed. The man that had taken me to the pinnacle and tossed me overboard was not a Lost Boy.

This was a man with skill and determination. What had I done?

I flipped over and gazed into Puck's lust filled eyes.

"We can't do this," I panted. "I was sleeping; I hadn't realized it was you."

The Puck I knew wouldn't have cared. He would have kissed me senselessly until I was begging for it.

But this new Puck only nodded and kissed my forehead.

"Good morning, Little Light," the rasp still in his voice. "We are leaving soon. Please get dressed and meet me on deck."

He slipped out of bed as I lay there in shock.

25

PUCK

My cock needed attention in the worst way. Not only had I survived sleeping next to the sexiest woman ever created as she tossed and turned, rubbing her heat all over me. But I'd walked away without pressing for more.

I knew that to win Tinkerbell I had to show her I was a changed man.

In the darkness of the hull, I wrapped my hand around my aching dick and stroked. It was her face, her mouth, and her eyes that came to mind as I pleasured myself. It had been this way for longer than I cared to remember.

I remembered how wet her pussy had been beneath my fingers. How soft her skin had felt, and how much I wanted to plow my cock into her heat.

My hand increased its speed as I pictured Tink underneath me, writhing with need and want as I wrapped her legs around my waist. Better yet, her lithe body riding on top of mine. Her full breasts bouncing with every thrust of my hips.

I wanted to see her lips wrapped around my length as she swallowed me whole.

My release was fast and hot as I pumped out the remainder of that fantasy. Once I had finished, I cleaned up and went on deck.

Everyone was assembled, and assignments were being given.

Ebony, Lily, and Pan were to head in from the north. Silver had a half dozen pirates guarding Ebony. Tink, Alex, Charlie and I were to take the southern route. That left Silver, Black Dog, Nate, and Tom to go around to the west since the village had the sea to the east.

We had sailed around to another spot on the Island where large cliffs had to be scaled before we could start our missions. It was decided that Peter and I would climb the cliff first so that we could secure the ropes for the others.

I ripped my shirt off and started up the rocks. There were plenty of footholds and rocks jutting out to make the climb. But I knew what my back would look like as my muscles worked to pull my body up the side of the cliff.

Tink had always had a weakness for my body and I was counting on her watching every muscle. I stretched, flexing my shoulders, reaching for a particularly difficult spot.

Peter was cursing me, as he followed in my wake. I wasn't worried about him. Hell, Peter was one tough mother fucker, who I had no desire to piss off. He would make it.

Once we reached the top we secured the ropes. We sent them down for the others to begin the climb.

"What was that about?" Peter threw a rock at my shoe and I smiled.

"Can't keep up, Old Man?"

He scoffed, "I just wasn't sure why we had to take the hardest route possible. Until I saw a certain fairy with her eyes glued to somebody's ass."

I perked up. "Really?"

Peter laughed. "You have it bad, my friend."

It felt good to be friends with Peter again. Sure, we weren't nearly as close as we once had been. But the hatred that he'd felt for me was no longer there. I only hoped that he never found out the real reason I'd enslaved Tinkerbell all those years ago. If that were to happen he would want my head.

When everyone had climbed the cliff. We broke off into our assignments and began to walk. On a map, Neverland doesn't seem as if it is a very large place. So, imagine my surprise when we were still walking five hours later and hadn't seen a soul.

I didn't want to complain and ruin Tink's image of me, but my feet had blisters on top of blisters and I was chafing something fierce.

I wanted to cast a spell to shore up my body, but I knew that the moment I used magic she would know. I was far more powerful than Tinkerbell, but any fairy could feel the shift in magic when it was used around them.

I hadn't realized that I was limping until Alex stopped the caravan.

"Tink," he rounded on her and I almost decked him until I heard his next words. "Your little joke is over."

She flushed, "I don't know what you are talking about."

Alex turned to me while running an impatient hand through his black curls, "Tinkerbell sprinkled all of us with pixie dust before the climb so that our bodies would be up for the walk. You obviously didn't have the same consideration. You are walking like your balls are raw and for the record, your feet are bleeding."

Tinkerbell let out a horrified gasp, "I didn't know that you were bleeding!"

I tried to change the subject, "It doesn't matter."

But it did. She had deliberately done this. I didn't know if she was trying to make me angry or punish me, but I knew how I needed to respond.

Without another word, I began walking again in the direction that we were assigned.

"That man has balls of steel," I heard Charlie whisper to Alex.

I didn't have balls of steel and I was certain that my feet were not the only area to be bleeding. But I wasn't going to give up on this one. I could have fixed it and most likely would. But I couldn't let Tinkerbell see that she'd hurt me.

It was another three hours before we saw smoke over the horizon.

We had come upon a stream and everyone had refilled their canteens. I gingerly put my feet in the water and hissed as the cold river soothed my torn flesh.

I felt someone approach, but I was too tired to turn around.

"I'm sorry."

Her whispered apology coated me better than any medicine. I looked up. "I'm not angry."

Tinkerbell looked hesitant. "I should have protected you. I was selfish and wanted to teach you a lesson."

I nodded. "I thought it might be something like that. You have every right to be upset with me. I suppose allowing me to get a true glimpse of what trekking through Neverland is like won't hurt me."

Her chin wobbled. "But it did hurt you."

I motioned for her to sit by me. "I have found that avoiding all the difficult parts of life has led me to leading a very dull existence. Sometimes one has to taste the pain to enjoy the pleasure, isn't that what the bard said?"

Her mouth lifted in a half smile. "Something like that. Puck, I don't understand what you are doing. I thought if I gave you enough time you would fly off the handle like you always do."

"Like I used to do," I gently corrected. "I am strong, Tinkerbell. I can withstand your challenges, if that is what you need to trust me again."

"I don't know if I will ever trust you." Her whispered words sliced through me, causing more pain than the arduous journey we had been on.

"I still have to try," I responded, as I looked out across the forest of Neverland wondering if I was a fool to have come here.

Lord knew that I was the king of fools in so many ways.

"Will you allow me to heal you?" she asked tentatively.

It was a task I could have easily done myself. But her willingness to help me touched something deep inside of my heart.

"Please," I muttered.

She walked over to me, her hands glowing bright with pixie dust. Tink started with my head and shoulders. She coated my chest and I felt the muscles easing and the pain diminishing. She stopped at my stomach and blushed as she brought her hands around to hold over my cock and balls.

The warmth from her hands combined with the healing dust had me groaning deep in my throat.

Tink swallowed hard and I saw her nipples pebble beneath her satin top. She stared into my eyes for a fraction too long and it was then that I knew she wasn't impervious to me. I still had a chance.

Slowly she made her way into the stream as she coated my legs and then my feet. I reached out and picked her up out of the stream. With a wave of my hand she was instantly dry.

Tink turned and before I could even think she kissed my cheek. "Thank you."

She turned and was off, and I was left there with a hard-on and the biggest smile to cross my face in centuries.

26

TINKERBELL

My lips tingled as I moved away from him. Why I had kissed him I hadn't the slightest idea. Charlie, of course, caught the entire event and was quick to jump on my ass.

"What's the story there, Tink?" His eyes were curiously intent.

"Just an old," I paused, because he hadn't been a friend. Lover, master, owner of my heart and soul; all these things described Puck perfectly, but I wasn't willing to share that. "Just an old acquaintance, that is all."

"Why do I get the impression that you are lying to me?" Charlie arched a brow, and I huffed, sinking down onto a fallen log to rest until we started up again.

"Charlie, just because we fooled around, it doesn't mean you have full access to my thoughts," I snapped.

His face remained impassive, and he sat beside me.

"I had rather thought that we were becoming friends. I noticed that you've stayed away from the boys and me lately. I hope we didn't offend you in any way."

I shook my head, "I'm sorry Charlie, we are friends. I am just sensitive when it comes to Puck."

"Do you love him?" His question startled me.

"Love him? Lord no! Loath, despise, and wary of him are better ways to describe how I feel," the words tumbled from my lips. But even as I said them, I knew that I wasn't completely honest.

"You did love him, then?" Charlie persisted.

I looked over to where Puck was sitting on the edge of the stream. His black hair was disheveled, and he had a fine layer of dirt from the trek through the forest. Instead of disgusting me, I felt a growl of possession so hot and instant that my nostrils flared. I had to get this under control before I found myself hopelessly lost under Puck's control.

"No," I whispered, but we both knew I was lying.

We marched along for another hour before we were close enough to see the Indian Camp. Puck devised a cloaking spell, and we split up, it was imperative that we stayed quiet.

Men were arguing, the Indian chief and a pirate. I had thought that we were the first group to reach the camp. But that dissolved when I heard Princess Tiger Lily join the fray.

We crept closer and saw that Ebony and Pan were tied to wooden stakes, their mouths had been gagged, but otherwise, they looked unharmed.

Lily was pleading with her father to let them go.

Something was wrong with the Indian chief. His eyes were glassy and unfocused. I felt Puck move closer and whisper into my ear.

"Enchantment?" his warm lips tickled my skin.

He was close enough that I could feel the heat of his body from my shoulders to my knees. I knew that he was only trying to be as silent as possible, but his nearness was wreaking havoc with my heart.

I nodded abruptly and went to speak, but he placed his finger gently across my lips and pointed to the camp.

My eyes followed his, and I saw that the pirates who had been assigned to Ebony were dead, slaughtered.

My gaze went back to Ebony, and I registered the pain in her eyes. Some of these men had been part of her crew, and others were new friends. Tiger Lily's father grabbed her hands and shouted in her face.

"If you do not wish to join your new friends," he spat on the ground, "You will cease this arguing immediately."

"Father?" Lily choked out, tugging her wrists, but his grasp was too firm.

"Take the Princess to her tent and see that she is properly guarded," the chief looked down at his daughter, and for a second, there was a concerned look on his wrinkled face. "It is for your protection."

Lily fought the pirate as he hauled her away, but the man was much stronger than the small girl. I looked behind us to where Alex was waiting, knowing that this would be torture for him.

But Alex was nowhere to be found.

Puck's hand settled on my waist, and it felt like a brand against my skin.

He leaned down again and whispered, "He's gone."

"Where?" I mouthed the word.

Puck shook his head as if to say that he didn't know. But things were not looking in our favor. I only hoped that Alex wouldn't do something incredibly stupid to get us all killed.

Charlie, who had been a few hundred yards to the right of where Puck and I were hiding motioned for us to fall back. Puck and I carefully retreated so that we could discuss our next move.

Once we were in a place where we could speak freely, Charlie filled us in on what he had seen.

"Every tribe member I saw had the same vacant expression," Charlie wiped his brow. "Whatever spell has been cast is affecting everyone in the vicinity. There are at least fifty men, if not more, preparing for battle."

"We need Peter and Ebony back," I bit my lip in concentration. "Charlie, did you see Hook or Silver?"

Charlie shook his head. "No. But I did see that the men were heavily armed."

I looked down at the small dagger that I had tucked into my belt and swallowed nervously. If there was to be a war, they would quickly demolish us.

Puck had come to the same conclusion, "We can't beat them, so we need to outsmart them."

Charlie, who wasn't the sharpest tool in the shed, wrinkled his brow, "How do we do that?"

"How many lost boys are on the Island?" I asked, remembering that we were not without resources.

Hangman's Tree wasn't far from where we were hiding, an hour at most.

Charlie brightened, "Thirty or so, I would say."

"Will you go there and gather as many as possible to fight?"

Charlie nodded, "Right away, Tink!"

I put my hand on his arm. "Make sure they know what they are getting into, Charlie. The younger ones need to stay behind."

Charlie rolled his eyes. "You sound like a mother hen, Tink. Don't worry. I've got this."

No one had ever accused me of being motherly. My cheeks heated. "Be careful, my friend."

Charlie grinned. "Always," and was off.

I turned to Puck who was eyeing me with a strange expression.

"What?" I felt my already hot cheeks burst again with color.

"Are you and that large fellow…" he broke off, "I apologize, it's none of my business."

The dejected note in his tone shocked the hell out of me. I suppose that is the only reason why I did what I did next.

I cupped his cheeks with my small hands. "I am not seeing Charlie. I won't lie to you and say that I haven't messed around."

I saw Puck's gaze harden.

"But that is long since over, and to be honest, was merely boredom."

Puck's violet eyes searched mine, and it was then that I realized I was touching his face. I could feel his whiskers pricking the delicate skin of my palm, and I immediately released him.

"I beg your pardon," I tried to step back, but Puck's arms curled around my waist faster than lightning.

"You do not need to apologize for touching me, Tinkerbell. You, of all people, can touch me anytime you like."

He leaned in, and for a terrifying moment, I thought he would kiss me. What was even more surprising, was that I wanted him to kiss me, desperately.

But he didn't. His eyes closed as he pressed his forehead against mine. Then his arms loosened, and he stepped back.

Clearing the gruffness from his throat, he added, "We had best keep an eye on Ebony and Peter, until Charlie and his band of lost boys return."

I nodded in agreement, but secretly, I was devastated that he hadn't taken things further.

Perhaps, I wasn't as immune to him as I wanted to believe.

27

PUCK

Weaving another spell of invisibility, Tinkerbell and I snuck into the camp with the intent of untying Peter and Ebony. Charlie had returned with twenty-seven boys from the ages of fourteen to twenty-five.

Four of the twenty-seven were near to wetting themselves, so we left them in the forest to watch over home base. Charlie and the other twenty-one armed themselves with bows, axes, and clubs. True, they were crude weapons, but it was the best they had. Armed and waiting they stood in the shadows, just outside of the Indian camp, awaiting the signal.

The moment we reached Peter and Ebony, I whispered into Peter's ear.

"Why are you hanging around here, mate?"

Peter blinked as if surprised and then a slow smile briefly flashed before dying.

He indicated his head toward Ebony, and I knew what he was asking.

"Tink," I whispered and then sliced through the ropes with my blade.

I gently placed a sword at Peter's side not wanting to disrupt their jailers. We were cloaked with the spell, and thankfully the sun had set at least an hour past.

Once they were untied, I snuck back around to the two men who had been guarding them. With a swift chop of my wrist, the first dropped to the ground. The second man bent over him.

"Mad Dog? What the hell are you…" but he wasn't able to finish his question as he joined his friend on the ground.

I felt Tink's presence. There was a need that always arose when she was near.

"Are they dead?"

"No," I grabbed her hand, and we made our way back to Peter and Ebony who had risen to their feet.

"It won't be long until they notice," Peter gripped the sword, "What is the plan?"

I waved my hand and removed the spell. This was the signal that Charlie and the boys had been waiting for. Quietly, they crept in to greet us.

"Find Hook," Ebony commanded, "Do not kill unless you have to."

I couldn't cover everyone with invisibility. There were too many. But I did cast a safety spell, whether it was wishful thinking or not remained to be seen.

With Tink's hand in mine, we crept along the outside of the camp. We hadn't gone far when we heard voices talking.

"She is my daughter, you cur!"

It was Silver.

The other man mocked him, "It would seem that you have a difficult time keeping track of the girl. She is my prisoner now."

Tink turned to me with wide eyes, "It's the Indian chief."

"How would you like Princess Tiger Lily tied to a stake?" Silver growled. "Ebony is of no use to you, Old Man. I have means. I can offer you gold and jewels. That is a far sight better than Hook will do."

The chief huffed, "My daughter betrayed me when she left with Ebony Hook."

Tink wrinkled her nose in confusion, "The chief loves Tiger Lily," she whispered.

He had to still be under some kind of spell or enchantment, all points leading to Captain Hook.

We heard a cry and then the sound of fighting. Someone had been discovered. The chief and Silver raced out of the teepee. Pirates and Indians alike were flooding the camp looking for the source of trouble.

"The prisoners have escaped!" another screamed, as swords clashed, and weapons sliced through the air.

The metallic smell of blood filled my nostrils, and the screams of dying men and women filled my ears.

I knew only one thing. I had to make sure that Tinkerbell survived this night.

I fought like a madman, and indeed I was filled with fire as I sliced and cut through those that tried to harm us.

I saw good men fall along with the others. I knew that we were outnumbered.

Tinkerbell fought by my side. There were only a few instances where someone got too close. We were covered in blood and mud, but much of it was not our own.

I saw Peter a few times as well as some of the others.

"STOP!" The command rang out louder than humanly possible, but the fighting continued.

"I WILL KILL HER!"

I then noticed who commanded us to stop. Hook had Princess Tiger Lily with a sharp blade to her throat.

It was strange how an entire battle could go silent in an instant.

The Indian chief cried out, "You promised her safety if I helped you!"

Hook's evil smile turned my stomach in disgust, "She can be safe in the next world, I guarantee it."

"Bastard," Tink whispered, and I was inclined to agree.

"Ebony!" Hook motioned for her to come forward. "You had one task, girl. And that was to kill the Pan."

Ebony tilted her chin up in defiance, "Am I your daughter?"

Hook's smile broadened, "I see you have been telling tales, Silver."

Long John Silver walked up, "James, it has been an age since I have seen you."

Ebony's jaw dropped, "This isn't a tea party!"

Silver ignored her, "Your fight is with me, James not that pretty little thing."

"Are you offering to take her place?" Hook raised a brow.

Silver chuckled, shaking his head, "Goodness, no! Slice the bitch's throat. It is of no concern to me."

Hook pressed the knife against Tiger Lily's perfect skin. A thin line of blood trailed down her neck.

"STOP!" Alex raced through the masses to get to Hook. "Do not harm her."

Hook rolled his eyes, "Smeed's boy."

I wasn't sure if Hook owned a looking glass because standing next to Alex there was no question of his parentage.

"Alex is your son," Ebony's tone was dangerously low. "Everyone here can see it."

Hook rolled his eyes, "Are you jealous? I assure you, there is no reason to be."

Alex swallowed looking pointedly at his father, "You admit it?"

"I dare say, I must have had dozens of children scattered about here or there."

"Release her," Alex moved a fraction closer, "I will do whatever you ask, just release her."

"You?" Hook scoffed, "You were told to keep Ebony safe. What did you do with my trust? You brought back the Jolly Roger along with the Henrietta, do you have any idea what you have done?"

Alex looked confused, and Ebony stepped forward.

"Take me instead, father."

Peter gasped and grabbed her arm, "The hell you will."

"You don't understand," Ebony said sadly. "We made a grave mistake."

Hook's smile widened, "You always were a bright girl."

"What are you talking about?" Peter demanded.

"Where did Silver go?" Hook's face turned dark, "Where is that bastard?"

Ebony shook Peter's hand from her arm and walked bravely up to Hook.

"The treasure," she put her hand on the blade hilt, and Hook allowed her to pull it away. "It contains the Never Stone, doesn't it?"

Hook shoved Tiger Lily into Alex's arms, "And now you have brought him here."

"Why is the Never Stone important?" Peter asked.

Ebony looked up, "It is what gives Neverland life. If he takes it, we all die."

I hauled Tinkerbell alongside me as I approached Hook.

"You are a right bastard!" I grit out.

He turned and twirled a long black curl, "A pleasure to meet you, as well."

Peter made the introductions, "This is Robin Goodfellow, but most know him as Puck."

Hook's eyes lit, "The trickster king?"

I inclined my head.

Hook turned to the crowd, "Burn the dead and gather yourselves. We are no longer on opposing sides."

There were a few murmurs, but they did as he said.

The Indian chief's gaze was no longer clouded as he approached his daughter.

"I did my part, Hook. We are not going to be involved in this war of yours."

Tiger Lily raised her head, the blood still drying on her neck.

"We are residents of Neverland. This attack is against us all. I will fight, Father, and so will our people."

28

TINKERBELL

I had my own place on the island, but it wasn't for the full-sized version of myself. So, I followed the group back to the makeshift base we had created. I could have stayed in the Indian village. Tiger Lily had graciously offered to anyone in need of a place to rest their head.

But a part of me wanted to be as far away from Hook as possible. He was a tricky bastard, and I still didn't believe his motives were purely to save Neverland.

There were too many holes in the story.

"What are you thinking about?"

I glanced away from the fire and saw Puck take a seat on a fallen log near mine.

"Hook," I saw no reason to lie, we were in this mess together. Whether or not I trusted him long term, that was another matter.

"I don't trust him," Puck said simply, "Why would he be angry at Ebony for not killing Pan and in the next breath accuse Silver?"

I shrugged, "I don't think Silver is innocent in all of this either."

Puck sat there for a moment, "Long John Silver is a man who is in it for himself. I have a feeling there is something large we are missing here. Something neither pirate wants us to know. But I cannot put my finger on it. Why does Hook hate Peter so badly?"

I shrugged, "Peter and Hook used to fight over the treasure. Each one, stealing it from the other and hiding it in a new location."

"What caused Peter to leave Neverland?"

Wendy, Michael, and John popped into my head.

"Peter was growing bored with the game. More and more, I found him leaving here and flitting around on earth. He even brought a girl and her brothers here for a time. When he took them back home again, he stayed there."

"He left you?" The incredulity in Puck's tone brought a smile to my lips.

"I don't think I factored into the equation," I murmured, looking back into the fire.

Puck frowned, "Why would he take you from me only to abandon you?"

I winced. I didn't want to remember those days. Not when I had been left behind by Peter, and I certainly didn't want to recall those times with Puck.

"It was a long time ago," I tried to play it off as if it didn't matter.

I hadn't realized back then, that I was so taken in by Puck. Peter had told me how controlling Puck was behaving towards me. It had chafed because I had thought we were something more than master and servant.

When I asked to go about more in fairyland, Puck had adamantly refused. He wouldn't say why, only that I was to obey him.

Those seeds of doubt had festered in my mind, and we argued more and more until I began to hate Puck. I wouldn't allow him to touch me and I certainly didn't obey him.

"Why?" I didn't realize that I had spoken, until Puck answered.

"Why, what?" he said gently.

"Why were you so controlling in fairyland?"

Puck stilled, his face turning to granite. "I was wrong, Tink. I am sorry, you don't know how sorry I am."

I nodded. "But that still doesn't explain why."

Puck ran a hand through his dark hair. "Must we rehash all of this?"

It was the closest I had seen him to losing his temper. I had to wonder if the old Puck was about to make an appearance.

"If you want me to understand and forgive you," I replied honestly.

Puck groaned and swore under his breath. "I fear you might hate me more, when you learn the whole of it."

"I suppose you will have to tell me and find out."

He stared. "Alright."

"You will tell me?" I felt my heart skip a beat.

He nodded. "Just let me tell the whole of it, before you pass judgment."

I agreed, and he began.

"You were working out in the forest the first time Oberon and I spied you. He was taken aback by your beauty and immediately commanded that you become one of his concubines. I convinced him that I would be the best person to claim you as his slave. I wove all kinds of lies about the guards taking you for themselves or being too rough with you."

My eyes widened, "You never claimed me for Oberon."

Puck swallowed, "My deceit was without boundaries, only that I couldn't allow him to take you. I told him whatever I needed to so that he would believe me. You see, I couldn't allow you to roam free in fairy, you were dead. And I took away your chance to be a favored concubine for the king. You could have lived in riches at the royal court and instead were confined to my chambers. I never told Peter the truth. He had noticed how secretive I had become. Peter had commented to the king that I wasn't myself, no longer whoring or drinking to excess."

My cheeks heated. I remembered many nights tangled in Puck's arms.

"And then Peter found out about you, he saw you through a boy's eyes. He threatened to tell the king I was abusing a slave. I was terrified that the king would find out about you. I had come to care for you so deeply that I thought I would die if I lost you. I suppose that should have been my first inkling that it wasn't meant to be. True love and the trickster king are not synonymous with each other."

"Why didn't you tell me?" I choked out.

Puck continued to stare at the fire. "We were fighting all of the time. I had come home in several instances and found you and Peter plotting and scheming. I know that he was a boy and I am a man. It wasn't sane. I was jealous. Goddess, I was so jealous that you wanted to spend time with him and not me. And then you were gone, Peter and you'd escaped."

By the time you both were discovered by Oberon, he had drawn his own conclusions. He blamed Peter for keeping you from him and faking your death. Oberon took away your full-size form and banished you along with him.

"And you kept silent?" I murmured, more to myself than to him.

"And I kept silent," his words were wrenched from him. "I thought you loved Peter. I was letting you go. I told myself that I had never loved you, for centuries I tried to convince myself that it was true."

"I never loved Peter," I turned to Puck, and he rested his violet eyes on my face.

"I know that now," he said sorrowfully. "I never should have taken you as my own. My actions got you kicked out of fairyland. I can understand if you can't forgive that."

"Puck," his name slipped out, like a prayer. "You should have trusted me."

He closed his eyes, regret covering his face.

"I don't hate you," the words tumbled out of me. "I was hurt and angry. I thought you were embarrassed by me, and that is why you kept me hidden away. I began to doubt everything. Peter knew that something wasn't right. I should have come to you instead of running. Puck, I would have hated being Oberon's concubine."

He opened his eyes, "Really?"

I took his face in my hands. His whiskers were gently abrading my palms.

"Are you claiming me? That saved me from being taken by a man that could never have loved me. All of the jewels and riches of the world wouldn't have changed the fact that I was a glorified prostitute for the king."

"Can you ever forgive me?" His plea shattered any remaining doubts that I had about this man.

I leaned forward and brushed my lips gently against his. A surge of heat swept through my belly, so fierce and insistent that I moved in for another kiss.

"I forgive you, Puck. Can you forgive me for leaving?"

His hands reached out and yanked me to him. My body was ablaze. I wanted this man, needed this man, and Goddess knew how desperately I loved him.

29

PUCK

Forgive her? What?

"Do you have any idea how much you mean to me? Fuck!"

Her delicate skin, flushed with desire, was hot under my fingertips. Visions of brighter days, with her in my arms, filled my mind.

"There is nothing to forgive, Tink, nothing."

Then without another thought, I took those sweet pink lips with my own and died a thousand deaths of sheer joy. Her mouth, there was nothing like the taste of her, heady like wine, sweet like fruit, and something intrinsically her.

Tink's small hands gripped my ass, and I growled in appreciation. She wasn't one to be shy while fucking and heaven knew that the fae had mastered the art over the centuries.

My tongue tangled with hers, and she moaned low in her throat. Those sounds, if I live another thousand years, I will never forget the sounds of pleasure that come from this woman. She nipped at my bottom lip, her mouth curving into a smile.

There was nothing that I wouldn't do for this woman. I wondered if she had any idea how far under her spell I truly was. I picked her up, and she wrapped her legs around my waist. I wanted to fuck her right then and there. But I could still hear camp, and she deserved better.

Tink curled her face into my neck as I walked further into the forest. There was a waterfall not far from where we had camped. At first, I had looked at the cave behind the falls to see if it would be a good base. But it was far too small.

However, for the two of us, it would be perfect.

Tink laughed when we came to the water, "I should have known."

I leered down at her, "That I would drag you to the nearest cave and fuck you senseless? Yes, you should have."

Her bubbling laughter went straight to my cock.

"No," she grinned. "That you would find Lovers Tryst."

My smile widened. "This place has a name?"

She rolled her beautiful eyes at me. "Everywhere in Neverland has a name, it's not that big of an island."

"It bloody well felt huge when we were trekking across it earlier!" I retorted, placing a kiss on the corner of her mouth.

"I am sorry about that," her eyes left mine for a moment.

I took her pointy chin in my hand and tipped her gaze to meet mine.

"No more apologies," I whispered.

She sank her hands into my hair and kissed me with a fierce determination that had my blood boiling. My hands dug into the globes of her ass. She was so damn soft where I was hard, sweet-scented, and all curves.

Tink tipped her head to the side as I placed hot, open mouth kisses along the curve of her neck. "Shit, Puck, that feels amazing."

Her voice was raspy and filled with need.

"I want to taste you," I murmured. "I want your cream on my tongue."

"Fuck," she breathed harshly.

I sat her on her feet, "Strip!"

Tink immediately obeyed, and I felt my cock harden even further. I hadn't thought it possible to be more aroused.

Once we were free of clothing, I picked her up again. The mist from the waterfall coated our heated bodies.

Lifting her up, I commanded that she wrap her legs around my head. Tink blushed wildly and did as she was told. Her sweet pussy was right where I wanted it.

I held her waist steady as she sank her fingers into my hair gripping tightly. I wasn't about to drop her.

I licked the seam of her core, and she was already wet, perfect.

"Spread your thighs as wide as you can," I commanded against her swollen flesh.

"Fuck, fuck, fuck!" Tink cried out, as I licked her with firm broad strokes.

She tasted like heaven, and I couldn't get enough of her. I buried my face in her core and ate her like a dying man at his last meal. I sucked her folds with my lips, gentle pulling.

Tink couldn't keep still. Her hips were rolling in a sensuous rhythm that gently fucked my face as I ate her. Her hands tightened on my hair and tugged to the point of pain.

I sucked her clit hard and nipped it with my teeth. She shattered on my tongue, and I drank the very essence of her.

Once I lifted her down, she blushed, "Your face!"

I smiled, knowing full well that her desire covered every inch of it.

"Best meal I have had in far too long to count," I grabbed my shirt and wiped my face and then turned back to her.

"On your knees," my voice was low and authoritative.

Her eyes automatically darkened, "May I taste you, Master?"

I felt my heart skip a beat. Could I handle her lips around my cock? It had been so long. I didn't want this to end before I had buried myself balls deep inside of her.

Tink had slipped to her knees. Her legs were slightly parted so that I could see the glistening folds of her pussy. Her breasts hung freely, beautiful in their rose-tipped glory. Tink kept her hands on her thighs, palms up, indicating that she was ready for instruction.

My cock was weeping precum, and I saw her lick her lips.

"Fuck, Tink, you are incredible. I wish you could see yourself right now. Your submission, it humbles me. I will protect you, love. I will honor you. I will do everything in my power to be worthy of the gift you freely give."

I walked up to her until my cock was level with her lips.

"Taste," I ran my length against her lips, coating them.

Tink's gaze met mine, and she licked her lips.

"You are the most beautiful creature," I placed my dick against her tongue. "Suck, my love."

She eagerly lapped at the head. Licking up every drop of precum and then swirling her tongue around the sensitive edge.

I gasped at the sensation. It was pure sin and bliss molded into one.

She pulled me further into her mouth, hollowing out her cheeks and sucking until my hands sank into her white-blonde hair. The little mewls of delights escaping her mouth sent ribbons of sensation through me.

Her dark blue eyes never left mine, and she sucked me deeper and deeper until I grazed the back of her throat.

"Fuck, Tink," I pumped my hips gently against her face, but I knew that she liked it harder.

Her hands tightened on her thighs, and I wondered if she would leave a mark.

"Touch yourself," I rasped. "Spread those thighs and I want to see your fingers playing with your pretty pussy."

She moaned as her fingers slid into her heat. And I saw it all. Every thrust of her hips, every flick of her wrist, every moan against my length, it was all mine.

I began to fuck her mouth, long deep strokes that had her growling in approval.

I pulled her upright when my dick was ready to burst. Placing her hands against the wall of the cave I cupped her firm ass with my hands.

"I love this ass," I whispered in her ear.

I pressed close enough that my dick rubbed against her ass cheeks. She moaned and pushed herself against my length.

"Where do you want it, Tinkerbell? I will let you decide."

She tossed her head back, and it landed on my shoulder.

"Whatever the master pleases," her eyes were glazed.

I reached up and pinched one of her nipples. It was hard enough to sting and leave a rosy glow.

"No, my love, it is you who will decide."

Her breath came out as a raspy moan when I pinched the other nipple. Both of her breasts were turning a lovely shade of pink.

I stepped back a fraction and ran my fingers along the crack of her ass. Bending her slightly, I traced the firm rosebud and felt her shudder.

"What do you want, Tinkerbell?" I asked firmly.

When she didn't respond, I smacked her ass. It jiggled from the impact, and a bright pink handprint appeared. I loved the look of my mark on her skin.

"You don't want me to choose, my love. Because I will fuck you until you can't walk in every hole and in every way."

"Yes," came the guttural cry, "Every hole, every way."

Fuck me.

30

TINKERBELL

I screamed as his cock rammed into my aching pussy. Puck wasn't small. It had been so long, too long. The pleasure was almost more than I could take. My body shook with need as he pulled out and rammed back inside of me.

I loved the way he dominated my body. He was the only one who could turn me on like this. His hands were punishing on my hips, as he whispered all the filthy things he wanted to do to me.

I knew he loved fucking my tits, and when his hands crept up my side and grabbed them, I moaned loudly.

"Oh, Tink," his voice had dropped to an unknown octave. One that sent shivers up my spine as he firmly molded my breasts.

Puck didn't do anything halfway. I can't say that we had ever had a quickie. He was all about the slow burn. I wouldn't be coming until I was begging for it.

His thick cock thrust into me in long steady strokes. I'd swear I could feel every bump and every ridge of his length. My jaw was sore from taking him all the way to the back of my throat, and I reveled in it. I wanted to be his.

He pulled out, and I couldn't help the involuntary cry that escaped my lips.

"Hold on, baby, you know I will take care of you, Little Light."

He would. Puck always kept his promises.

He laid me down on the smooth cave floor. It was cold and a bit damp, feeling incredible against my inflamed skin. Throwing my arms above my head he commanded I hold them there, so I nodded, doing as I was told.

There had never been a time when he had gone too far. I trusted him implicitly in this respect. If I said stop, it would indeed stop.

He picked up my hips for another quick taste, "I can't help myself. Your scent calls to me."

I loved the way Puck wasn't afraid to tell me how he felt.

Suddenly, the cave was illuminated with bright sparkling light. I had thought that it came from him until I saw his look of pride. I couldn't help the flush that spread across my chest, covering all the way to my nipples and up to my cheekbones.

"You are my Little Light," Puck growled, and lifted my left leg before sliding into my pussy once again.

It was deeper this way and couldn't hold back the whimpers.

"More, Master, please!"

A wicked smile crossed his handsome face. "More?"

He thrust inside of me so hard that I saw stars. My core clenched hard around him, and I was rewarded with a growl of approval from his handsome lips.

Puck fucked me relentlessly. His strokes were fast and hard as my back arched off the cave floor. My fingers grasped at the cool stone, finding no purchase.

He took my left leg and crossed it over the right. I could feel him all the way to my womb, and he slid in once again fucking me sideways.

"You are so fucking tight, Tink," sweat dripped from his brow, and I could see his skin glistening in the fairy light.

I was close but didn't want to come without him. Puck had other ideas though.

He rammed into me, repeatedly as I tried to hold on.

Then I began to plead, "Master, I'm going to cum!"

The fierce look of possession that crossed his face, along with a particularly hard thrust, and I was coming.

"Cum, Little Light! All over my cock, cum!"

I couldn't have stopped myself. It was so powerful and intense that black dots appeared in front of my eyes. I was powerless, as my pleasure soaked every inch of my body.

Puck pulled out and moved my left leg back so that I was exposed to him. His length was impossibly aroused, looking angry and purple in the fairy light.

He gathered my pleasure on his fingers and traced them down to my ass. Fingering the tightness there he gently began to play, and I felt my lower stomach clench.

The moment his fingertip entered my ass I cried out with need. It was just a bit painful and a thousand times naughty which only enhanced my desire to have him take me in every way.

My body was afire, and I was begging and pleading with him.

"Please, Master, fuck my ass, take me, please!"

His violet eyes had deepened, as he responded, "You are mine, Little Light. There will be no more, only me."

I nodded, and I meant it. No other man could make me feel this way, make me respond this way.

He sank a finger inside of my ass, and I groaned. Puck was careful to make sure that I was ready. It had been a long time since I had allowed anyone to take me this way.

One finger became two and then finally three. It was tight, and I winced at the pleasurable pain that radiated from my bottom.

I felt the head of his cock, weeping with need at the entrance of my little hole. I tried to shove myself against it, but Puck was in charge, not me. I felt a sharp slap on my thigh near the bottom of my ass.

"Wait, my love, I don't want to hurt you."

"You couldn't hurt me," I moaned, "You wouldn't hurt me."

At that moment, I realized it was true. Puck had never hurt me. He had been controlling and secretive, but he had never laid a hand or spoken a cruel word to her. He could be devastatingly cruel, he was the king of tricksters, after all.

"I love you, Master," the words came out unbidden, and Puck stopped.

His thick cock right where I wanted it. Then he was inside of me, shoving his massive length and filling my ass until I couldn't breathe.

"I love you, Tinkerbell, with all that I am. I promise to forsake all others. I will honor, care, and love you until the end of my days."

With those words, my heart seized inside of my chest. He had just recited to me the fairy coupling vow.

He was still inside of me, filling me so full that I ached with it.

"I love you, Puck, with all that I am. I promise to forsake all others. I will honor, care, and love you until the end of my days."

There was a flash of light, and the coupling was forged. Our words were creating an impenetrable bond that couldn't be broken. It was an old custom, one that hadn't been used for thousands of years. The fact that he had not only… bound me to him in this life but also the one beyond, wasn't lost on me.

"Do not cry, Little Light," he rasped.

"Take me, my love!" I begged. "This is only happiness, Master. I need you."

The moment the words were out, Puck began to fuck my ass, sliding in and out with speed and precision. Heat, which had already bloomed in my lower abdomen, spread throughout my entire body.

His dick rammed into me again and again, as he spread the lips of my pussy. Thrusting his fingers deep inside of me, he finger-fucked my core as he fucked my ass.

He growled long and loud as my pussy clenched his fingers. He was close, I knew it.

"Cum, Little Light! I need you to cum, my love!"

My body immediately obeyed as my orgasm ripped through me. I was shaking as he pumped two more times before filling my ass with his seed.

I was thoroughly sated and hardly noticed when he whispered

something about loving the sight of his cum leaking from my ass. Puck loved to talk during sex, and I loved to hear what he had to say.

He gathered me into his arms and cradled me close. I felt safe and protected. He was mine, and I was his.

We sat that way for several moments. Perhaps even half an hour, as I breathed in the scent of him and marveled at how right this was. I belonged to him, I always had.

"What are you thinking about, Little Light?"

His question startled me, but I answered honestly.

"You do belong to me, Tink. Just as I belong to you," He kissed the side of my head, and I sighed in contentment.

"What are you thinking about?" I asked, and he smiled against my skin.

"I have a crazy idea that just might work.," He pulled back enough to see my face.

I reached up to cradle his jaw. "If anyone can help, it is you."

He kissed my palm.

I knew the trickster king was back.

31

TIGER LILY

"If it comes to swinging, swing all, say I."

-Robert Lewis Stevenson, Treasure Island

I was raised to honor and respect my elders, to not question authority, and to do as I was bid. But I was also raised to stand up for what was right, even when it was the difficult choice. My father was the strongest man I had ever known.

I had never been more disappointed with anyone in my entire life, as I was tonight with him.

"How dare you contradict my word, girl?" His eyes were blazing with indignation.

I should be thankful that the poppy he had smoked has worn off enough that he seemed somewhat in the present. It had become an addiction to him over the years.

"Our people deserve the right to fight for the land they live on," I said simply.

I didn't care that my father's face was bright red or that he spat a little when he yelled. I had witnessed his temper all my life. But I had never seen him cower away from what was right.

"You would lead our people to their deaths?" Arms flying, he continued, "It will be a mass slaughter. Forever they will lament your choices, Tiger Lily. You were the one who ordered their demise."

What was clear to me was that he hadn't contradicted me in front of the people. He knew, deep down, that this was the right choice. But in his old age, the drugs had become more of a reality that even I was.

"There wouldn't be a forever, father. If the Never Stone leaves the island, everyone will die. We have all lived beyond normal life expectancies. We fight, and we might have a chance. Yes, it is possible that we will not win. I do not deny that. But if we don't fight, we have assured our deaths."

His cheeks puffed out, "You are only a woman, what do you know about war?"

I had to take a deep breath, and then several more.

"Did you even notice that I was gone all these months? Or were you too busy smoking your pipe and having *visions*?"

He raised his hand for the first time ever in my presence.

"Are you going to hit me?" my tone was deceptively quiet. "Go ahead, if that is how you believe I should be treated. I won't stop you."

He stepped back, surprised at his own actions, "I would never hit you."

My brow furrowed, "You aren't the man that raised me. He was brave and knew how to lead his people. He would never have allowed Hook to take over the camp."

There was a moment of heavy silence. I saw the fine lines on my father's face and the stoop to his shoulders. Most people didn't age past twenty-five in Neverland. But there were some that the aging process only slowed but didn't stop.

I have no idea what the difference is and how to stop myself from being the latter. A niggling of doubt crept into my thoughts. It did seem as though the individuals that aged; Hook, Smead, and my father were all men that at times walked the wrong side of good and evil.

I had a strong hunch that there was a correlation.

Someone cleared their throat, and then asked permission to enter the tent.

Alex.

I felt my heart gallop at the mere sight of the handsome pirate who resembled a Latin Lothario. His black curly hair touched his shoulders, and my fingers ached to touch those springy locks.

His chiseled jaw looked to be made of granite; and his eyes, almost black in color, were warm on my face.

Alex was much taller than I was and must have had another hundred pounds on his frame of sheer muscle. I loved his tan skin and shockingly white teeth. Everything about him sent shivers up and down my spine.

But I couldn't let him know. Life was complicated enough as it was.

"What do you want, boy?"

My father could be such a charmer.

"Alex, please come inside," My smile widened when I caught his shy crooked one.

Damn, that boy was positively lickable.

Alex turned to my father, "I beg your pardon, Chief. But Captain Hook wishes to know if he can count on the tribe's support?"

"Bastard," my father spat on the ground, and I saw Alex's jaw tighten.

I glared at my father. This was his moment of truth. Was he still the honorable man and chief of the tribe that he had once been?

"Ask Tiger Lily," my father mocked. "She will be leading this lunacy."

A sigh of relief escaped my lips, but at the same time, an arrow of sorrow pierced my heart.

I turned to Alex. "You may take me Captain Hook, Mr. Smead. I will speak with him about the tribe's involvement."

Alex nodded and offered a short bow to my father that was borderline disrespectful. It was, sadly, more than he deserved.

"WAIT," I stared in disbelief, "You don't know where the treasure or the Never Stone is located?"

Hook sneered at me, "Do you honestly believe that I would still be on the island if I had found that treasure?"

"So, you are no better than Captain Silver? Why would we help you?"

Alex took a step closer to me at the same time Hook raised his arm with the severed hand. The sharp hook glistened in the light from the fire. It was menacing as well as oddly magnificent.

"I have no desire to steal the Never Stone, Princess," Hook twirled his mustache with the silver instrument. "But I would like that treasure. I am still a pirate, Milady."

"What is your plan, Captain?" I was willing to hear what he had to say, but there was no way that I was letting him walk off with any treasure. For all we knew, the gold and the Never Stone wouldn't work without each other.

"I need you and Alexander to approach the Mermaids in Mermaid Lagoon. They despise the pirates, but I know they have a fondness for his pretty face."

Alex flushed, as a scowl broke out.

I stifled a grin. "Very well. What is the goal of this mission?"

"Their lagoon is rife with buried treasure," Alex muttered. "But as far as we know it is nothing compared to Silver's treasure."

Hook nodded, "Just as the boy says. However, you are looking for something." He leaned in close. "The leader, Atlantia was entrusted with the map to the treasure. We need that map."

"And you think that she will give it to Alex and me?" I shook my head, "There is no love lost between the Indian Tribes and the merpeople. I don't think they will hand anything over willingly."

Hook's eyes glinted, and for a moment he looked startlingly like Alex.

"I never said they would hand it over, Princess. Make no mistake. It will be hard fought. I am sending the boy as protection. But he is also one of the best thieves on the island. My daughter wouldn't lie about these things."

Alex gritted his teeth.

Ebony wasn't his true daughter, and yet Hook still claimed her? His own son stood directly in front of his face and Hook called him *the boy*?

"We need that map, tomorrow, if not yesterday."

I nodded in agreement. "I will travel with your son to the merpeople. We will return with the map."

Hook's eyes narrowed, "You are a brave woman, Princess Tiger Lily."

I didn't know if he was referring to my use of Alex's parentage or the fact that I had assured him of the success of our mission. I didn't stop to ask either, and I grabbed Alex's arm in a firm hold as I exited the tent.

We walked in silence for a time as we passed the other tents and moved towards the forest. I heard a branch snap and turned to see who was approaching when Alex shoved me up against a tree. The movement was so quick. I let out a startled squeal of protest.

"Is there anyone there?" I heard one of the pirates from Ebony's crew call out.

"It is only me, Alex," he replied, his body covering mine fully. "I had to take a piss."

My cheeks heated at the thought of his cock out in the open, even if Alex had been rather crass.

"No worries, mate, I will see you on the morrow." The sound of footsteps departing left Alex and me still glued to each other.

With the tree at my back, I could hardly breathe. His breath caressed my face, and I smelled a hint of rum on his breath. My lips twitched; Alex was a true pirate to the core.

"I believe we can separate now." My voice was breathier than I had imagined it would be.

Alex grunted, "No, we can't."

"Why?" My brow furrowed, but his answer came in the form of a kiss. Everything I thought I knew about life was suddenly turned to its end.

Damn, the man knew how to kiss a woman.

32

TIGER LILY

His lips were firm as they slanted over mine demanding entry.

I had been kissed before. Indeed, Peter had planted one on me when he was younger. I remember the pleasant feeling of a boy's lips touching mine and that pit of warmth in my stomach.

Kissing Alex was nothing like kissing a boy.

My core clenched with need as he plundered my mouth, possession, and danger in every swipe of his tongue. My legs trembled beneath me. I might have fallen, if Alex hadn't pressed me harder against the bark of the tree.

My thin leather dress left nothing to the imagination as he pressed his massive cock against my belly. I didn't have a warm, comfortable feeling there. No, this was more of an inferno that threatened to burn me alive.

"Touch me!" Alex demanded, and I realized that I was so wrapped up in the kiss that my arms were lying by my side. I gingerly lifted them up and touched the naked skin that was bared by the neck of his shirt.

We both moaned as my fingers stroked his skin. He was every bit as hot as I was, and that only served to embolden me.

I touched his muscular pecs and ran the tip of my finger over his flat nipple through his shirt.

Alex growled and bit my lower lip tugging at it, "You are playing with fire, little girl."

"I am already burning!"

His eyes widened at my admission. He kissed me again, as if he couldn't help it, as if he would die if he couldn't taste me one last time. The firestorm of emotion enveloped both of us. We couldn't get enough of each other.

Tongues and teeth mashed as he tilted my head back so that he could delve further. I knew that he wanted to conquer me, and I was far from giving him a reason not to.

My fingers dug into his abs, and I wanted to touch his naked skin, but I wasn't quite brave enough.

His hands had remained on my waist and ass, almost as if he were forcing himself to stay still.

I was about to demand that he touched me like I was doing to him when Alex wrenched his lips away.

"I will not apologize," he warned, as his glittering eyes raked my body.

I felt naked under his gaze, naked and wanton.

I wanted to flippantly reply that I hadn't asked for a damn apology, but then something better came to mind.

"I won't fucking apologize either!"

Alex's eyes widened at the curse word, and I saw him take a step forward and then mentally battling with himself.

This man wanted me, and I wanted him.

I didn't know what internal battles he was struggling with. But I was tired of the dance that we had been doing around each other all those months of the voyage. I knew that I was innocent in comparison to Alex.

I hadn't experienced pleasures of the flesh to the degree that he had. Being the chief's daughter had a way of keeping one innocent. The men in my tribe liked their scalps where the gods had put them and not on my father's belt.

"I will take what I want from you Alex Smead," I continued. "You are a big boy. If you don't care about my advances, you are going to have to fight me off."

He sputtered, dumbfounded, "You, are going to ravish me?"

I shrugged. "If I want to I will, and if you are really lucky."

Alex stumbled back a bit, and then out of nowhere smacked his forehead rather harshly.

"Damn it, fuck!"

"What is the matter with you?" I demanded, pulling his hand away and looking at the red mark that was blossoming on his face.

"Waking myself up," he grumbled. "Or at least trying to."

I laughed. I couldn't help myself.

"Come along, Sleeping Beauty," I teased, as I began to walk in the direction of Mermaid Lagoon.

Alex stared at me for a moment or two before launching himself forward, grumbling under his breath.

My heart seemed lighter as we walked in silence. The night was coming on, but I had grown up in these forests and knew where the best places to sleep were. I could tell that Alex wasn't used to it by the way he spooked at every sound.

"It is only the toads singing," my lips were behaving traitorously. "You have nothing to be afraid of, Mr. Smead."

Alex looked indignant, "I am not afraid, Lily!"

It warmed my heart that he called me by my nickname, and not Princess Tiger Lily.

"I will protect you, Alex," and I would with my dying breath.

In an instant, he had his arms around me, and I couldn't move an inch. I felt the heat from his hard body and knew that I was in trouble.

"What are you doing?" I hissed, but he placed a hand over my mouth. I almost argued, but then I heard it, men talking.

"We need the girl for ransom, Silver," Black Dog said gruffly, "You should never have let the bitch go."

There was a low murmur that I couldn't make out, and then Silver spoke, "We need them to lead us to the map. If I know Hook, he is desperate to find it before we do. Why do all the work when he will do it for us?"

A squeaky parrot squawked, and there was a rustling noise.

"I am going to kill the bastard if he gives us away," Black Dog growled in annoyance. "He's just a damn bird!"

"Damn bird! Damn bird!" was the parroted reply.

"Have the spies returned with information?" Silver ignored them both.

"Not yet," Black Dog replied. "But I expect them any second."

I felt Alex pick me up and then throw me over his shoulder. Then to my utter shock and horror, he walked right into Silver's camp.

"I have news and a hostage," he set me down none too gently and began tying my wrists and feet.

"Are you fucking kidding me?" I cried out, fighting him with everything I was worth.

"You were to bring my daughter," Silver's sword glinted in the firelight.

"She wasn't there," Alex pulled the ropes tight enough to bite.

"How could you betray me?" I shrieked, but anything else was muffled by the handkerchief that Alex shoved into my mouth.

"But I have the location of the map," his eyes glanced at mine, and there was something there that I couldn't quite understand. I hated him more than anyone else in the world at that moment. I had trusted Alex. I was halfway to falling in love with the man.

I willed the tears that threatened to fall back. I wouldn't let him see me cry, not if the world depended on it.

Silver and Alex spoke late into the night. I was offered something to eat, but I refused. Alex did force some water down my throat, but he succeeded in soaking my dress in the process. As the night grew later, I began to shiver. We had never made it to a cave and the night wind was cold against my wet clothing.

I felt myself being yanked from the chair I had been tied to. My feet were quickly tied again, but Alex had pulled me close to where he was lying.

"I will remove the gag if you promise not to yell. One word and it goes back in; do you understand?"

I nodded slowly and then whimpered as he pulled out the offending cloth. True to my promise I didn't speak a word. Not when he shared the blanket to soothe my chills, not when my eyes finally found sleep, and certainly not when my fingers found the hilt to his blade in the early morning.

33

ALEX

I felt the tip of a dagger at my throat and almost smiled. Tiger Lily never ceased to amaze me.

"Are you going to run me through?"

I hadn't opened my eyes yet, and my voice was laced with sleep.

"Give me one good reason not to," Tiger Lily pressed the dagger deeper, and I felt the slightest of pinches.

"Giving me a scar will only increase my good looks," I opened my eyes and smiled at her. "You are so damn beautiful."

Tiger Lily growled, "That isn't a good reason."

I raised a brow, lips twitching. "No, I suppose you are right. How about this? We need Silver's scuba diving gear to find the map. Unless you have a way for us to breathe underwater? If that is the case, then we shall make our escape now."

Her eyes blazed for the briefest of moments, before she pulled the dagger away from my throat.

"Why didn't you tell me?"

I glanced around camp to see if anyone was paying attention to us. It was still early. The sun hadn't broken across the sky.

Leaning in and whispering into her ear, "I was too busy kissing your mouth, tasting your passion, and picturing you naked and writhing beneath me."

The dagger was back at my throat in an instant.

"Do you think this is a game, Mr. Smead?" Tiger Lily looked every inch the princess that I knew her to be.

"No, my lady," I answered solemnly. "But I do seem to get my priorities confused when my tongue is tangled with yours. I humbly apologize."

She grunted, it was the most ladylike grunt I had ever heard, and a wide smile split my face. Tiger Lily lowered the dagger, and I wrapped my fingers around hers at the hilt so that she couldn't accidentally separate my head from my shoulders.

I had grown rather fond of its current placement.

"I don't like being the hostage," Tiger Lily murmured.

I couldn't blame her for it. I had been held captive a time or two. Your arms begin to ache after about an hour, and then another hour after that they become numb. The ropes burn into your skin, and you find yourself tugging at them, even though you know full well that they aren't going to unravel themselves.

"I can't untie you, Princess," I whispered into her ear.

She snuggled up under my chin, and I felt the smooth stands of her dark hair caress my skin.

"Try and get some sleep. We have a long walk ahead of us."

I began to stroke her back, and after a short time, her eyelids began to droop. I lay awake and watched her as the sun began to peek over the mountaintop. Her smooth tanned skin hadn't a blemish in sight. I loved the way her pouty lips parted as she sighed.

I had wanted this woman for as long as I could remember. But I hadn't truly gained respect for her until our journey. When you love someone from afar, you tend to gift them with attributes you wish them to have.

Often, the real person isn't anything like the illusion you have conjured in your head. Tiger Lily wasn't a bit like I had thought she would be. The reality far outweighed anything I could have dreamed up.

Her kind spirit and loving nature as she took Ebony under her wing, surprised me. Her valiant heart and strength of character as we merged crews with Silver's, impressed me. But her determination to do right by her people and Neverland, endeared her to me far more than anything else.

Tiger Lily's eyes flickered open the moment some of the pirates began walking around camp. I pressed a quick kiss to her lips before sitting up and hauling her up beside me.

In a gruff voice, I said loud enough for the others to hear that I needed to take a piss and that she was welcome to do the same.

I saw her lip curl in disdain. I knew she didn't like my pirate persona, but I had to keep up appearances. I cut the rope securing her feet together, and we walked away from the group. As soon as I could, I sliced the rope at her hands and rubbed the aching skin as blood flooded back into her limbs.

Giving Tiger Lily a moment of privacy, I did indeed take a piss. Once I had relieved myself, I waited for her to return. She was back moments later with a bright blush on her cheeks. We walked to the stream and washed our hands off.

"I need to tie your wrists again," I said with regret.

Tiger Lily didn't fight me or even complain. That was just one more thing that I had to add to my list of things I admired about her.

The crew broke camp, and we began the hike through the woods to the shoreline. Thankfully we weren't as far away as some of the other groups had been. After a few hours, we reached the beach and loaded the boats.

Soon we were back aboard the Henrietta. Silver wanted Tiger Lily to be strapped to the main hull, but I refused.

I didn't see any reason why she couldn't be confined to a cabin. That way she wouldn't have to be tied up, but I didn't voice this to Captain Silver.

With a grunt, he agreed to my request, and I took her to the room that Ebony had occupied on the ship. It was the second-best cabin, besides Captain's Quarters.

The moment we opened the door I could almost smell Ebony's perfume. I loved her, but not as a man loves a woman. Ebony and I were always the best of friends, and I grew up most of my life thinking that she was my half-sister.

It wasn't until later that I learned she was Silver's daughter and not Hook's.

I barred the door and again sliced the bands that held her wrists.

"Thank you," Tiger Lily rubbed the sore skin, and I lifted her hands so that I could place a small kiss on the reddened flesh.

"I am so very sorry," I muttered, hating the way that she flinched when my lips touched her.

A ghost of a smile crossed her face, "It isn't your fault. You tied the ropes so loosely the last time I could almost slip free of them."

I felt heat crawling up the back of my neck, "I don't wish to hurt you at all."

She nodded, "I know, and I admire you for that."

The blush spread, and I felt ten times the fool. Trying to impress her, I attempted to swing around the chair and offer her a seat. But the chair, which I should have known, was bolted to the cabin floor. So instead of swinging the chair around, I ended up wrenching my arms and stumbling backward, until I landed on my ass.

"Are you alright?" I could tell that she was trying to hold back her laughter, but there was genuine concern in her eyes.

Grinning ruefully, I answered, "That is what I get for trying to be a gentleman when I am clearly not one."

A giggle escaped Tiger Lily's perfect lips.

"Most ladies would agree that a dashing pirate is far more desirable than a stuffy old gentleman anyway."

Her hand rested gently on my head, and I felt her fingers brush through the black curls.

I didn't think about it or hesitate for even a moment. If she wanted a pirate, she had come to the right place.

I snatched Tiger Lily by the waist and pulled her down into my lap. Her leather dress split up the side as her thighs stretched out over mine.

All that smooth, perfect skin was more than I could take. And thoughts of being a gentleman had clearly fled my mind.

"Mine!" I growled as I bent to kiss her. But she lifted a finger to my lips to stop me.

Then to my surprise, she trailed the finger down past my chin to the center of my chest. My breath was coming in rapid pants, and I knew that she had to feel the hardening of my cock beneath her perfect ass.

Pressing into my skin, she whispered, "Mine!"

And I was lost.

34

TIGER LILY

The slightly feral look in his eyes only encouraged me further. I slipped each button free exposing more and more of Alex's broad chest. I had heard rumors about him. Rumors that made my panties wet and my core ache with need.

There were whispers of his need to dominate in the bedroom. I wished that I wasn't so innocent, that I knew more about pleasing a man. His hands rested on my thighs and then slid up to cup my ass. His fingers played with the lace edge of my panties driving me crazy with lust and need.

I could feel his cock, long and hard underneath me. I couldn't help rubbing myself against it.

He growled low in his throat, "Tiger Lily, I will give you one chance to end this."

The veins in his neck stood at attention and I could see the muscle clench in his jaw.

"Take me, Alex, don't hold back."

He cursed vilely, "Fuck, you don't know what you are asking."

His fingers dug into the plump flesh of my ass and I knew that he was holding on by a thread.

"I've heard things," I whispered in his ear, before licking the shell with the tip of my tongue.

Alex's breath caught, and, in an instant, he had me tossed over his knee. My hands flew out to grab the legs of the chair and I felt the cool breeze on my ass as he lifted the torn leather skirt.

His hands caressed the globes of my ass tenderly, almost reverently. I felt exposed and knew that if he could see my face it would be seven shades of red.

"I want to spank this ass," he said darkly. "Does that frighten you?"

I felt my pussy pulse at his words, "No, I am not scared."

"I want to tie you up in knots, so that when I fuck you the only thing you can do is scream my name as you come repeatedly."

I could feel the heat of his cock, and it throbbed as he told me what he wanted to do with my body.

"Tiger Lily, you should have walked away when you could," he rasped.

I raised my ass up in defiance, "I can take anything you dish out."

There was a loud crack and then heat seared through my bottom. I couldn't help the yelp of surprise that escaped my lips.

He brought his hand down again and I squirmed in his lap.

"Is it too much for you, Little Princess?"

Alex's words were like a caress. Then he pulled my panties down my thighs, and I felt the air kiss my heated skin.

His fingers found the juncture of my thighs and I heard the smile in his voice when he praised me.

"Little Princess, you are soaked. I have never seen such beautiful skin before. You are perfect, and you are mine."

I felt his long fingers rub across my delicate folds and I shivered in response to his touch.

Another smack and I tensed for a moment waiting for the sting to subside and the feeling of warmth to take over. His fingers dipped between my ass cheeks after every smack. The juices began to run out of my pussy, soaking my inner thighs.

I wanted him… needed him, but I knew that he was in charge of my pleasure. At long last he picked me up and cradled me in his arms.

"You did so well, Lily," Alex kissed every inch of my face while holding me against his vast chest. "I am so proud of you."

He picked me up and carried me over the bunk. There he helped me out of my dress and I realized that my panties had already fallen off sometime during the spanking.

Alex took a strip of cloth and wound it around my head.

"I don't want to bind your wrists again, because they are sore. But I do want you to hold on to the bars on the top of the bed. Can you do that?"

I nodded breathlessly.

But Alex pinched my nipple. "I need words, Lily."

"Yes," my voice was gravelly with need. "I will hold on."

"Good girl," he stoked my body with light touches.

Without my sight, everything felt more intense. From the burning of my bottom against the bedsheets, to his lips against the hollow of my throat, I felt love in every touch. His fingertips traced the ridges of my ribcage right before his tongue followed the same path. He was seducing me, and I was powerless to withstand him.

A keen cry escaped my lips the moment he sucked my nipple into his mouth. The suction seemed to zip through my breasts and have a direct link to my core. My hips arched as I whimpered, digging my fingers into the bedpost so that I wouldn't be tempted to wrap them in his long black locks.

His hot mouth teased and played with my nipples pulling on them and sucking deep until I couldn't think, couldn't reason.

I was pleading with Alex to help ease the ache between my thighs. It was unbearable the pressure that had gathered there, I needed relief.

I felt his large hands on my knees and the rush of cool air against my fevered flush.

"Shit, I need you. Please Alex, I need you."

I wasn't even sure what I was begging for, only that he had the answer to what my body needed. I felt him blow against my folds and I blushed knowing that he was seeing the very heart of me. No man had ever lain between my thighs. When I felt his fingers part my pussy I moaned low in my throat.

Alex growled and nipped at my inner thigh.

"Do you have any idea how fucking sexy you are? How your smell is forever imprinting itself in my brain? There will never be another woman that could possibly live up to the reality of who you are."

His fingers brushed against my swollen folds, "And your taste... Fuck, Lily, I have to taste you."

He brought his mouth to my pussy and licked my core. I felt as if a million fireworks had gone off in my stomach. My pussy throbbed and wept as he stroked his broad tongue over me, through me, and into me.

My body writhed until Alex had to grab hold of my hips to keep me still. He buried his face into my heat, licking and sucking.

Alex was doing wild and wicked things to my body and I never, ever, wanted him to stop. I pleaded for more and screamed out his name along with every other naughty obscenity that I had ever heard.

He chuckled against my flesh, his whiskered chin abrading my tender skin. I was close, so close to coming harder than I had ever come in my life. My innocent touches had never driven the maelstrom of emotion that this man could with his mouth.

His finger slid deep inside of me as he sucked my clit into this mouth and I shattered. Screams pouring from my mouth as my hips jutted against his face. I didn't have control and couldn't have known the power of such an orgasm. My body continued to clench as he stroked me thought that orgasm.

Then to my surprise, his fingers began to play once again on my already sensitive flesh. I begged him to give me a moment. But Alex was relentless. When his lips joined his fingers, he sent me flying once again.

My body felt as though I had run a marathon. I could hardly

gather air into my lungs when I felt the bands of my blindfold being loosened.

"I," my eyes were wild. "You, and then your mouth. Shit, Alex, how? Is it always that way?"

He stilled, and I worried that I had said something wrong, done something wrong.

"What is it?" I grasped at his open shirt. His closed expression was scaring me.

"Tiger Lily," he began, and my heart sank at the sound of my full name. He had called me Lily before and even Little Princess. I didn't want him to see me as Tiger Lily.

"Lily," I demanded, with a certain stubbornness to my chin.

I caught something in his eyes, but it was gone as quickly as it came.

"Have you done this before?" Alex demanded.

I tried to hedge, "Have I done what before?"

"Damn it all to hell, Lily! Are you a virgin?"

My blush was all the answer he needed. In a second, he had ripped himself away from me.

"Fucking hell! Fucking, fucking hell!"

He raked his hands through his hair. "I would have been tender, shit, Lily. I spanked you for fuck's sake!"

My eyes grew wide. "Would you rather I had lain with a man? Because I can try and rectify that situation for you!"

In hindsight, I really shouldn't have poked the beast.

35

ALEX

Tiger Lily was bared and spread before me as she taunted me with words about another man. My possessive side knew that this woman was mine and mine alone. I would never allow her to be with anyone else.

Did she not realize that when I told her to walk away, I meant—forever? I didn't do girlfriends. Hell, I rarely had a woman more than once. I didn't want to create any situations where the lady thought it was anything more than fucking.

But not with Tiger Lily, never with her. I wanted every morning, the fluttering of her eyelashes as she awakened. I wanted every night, her passionate body given freely in submission as I guided her to new and exciting heights of pleasure. I wanted her daytime, her words, her wisdom, and her laughter.

I wanted her.

"There will not be any other men," I growled.

Her brow rose, "Really?"

"I told you. You're mine, and you claimed me for your own."

Tiger Lily drew in a harsh breath, and I felt my heart begin to race.

"What are you saying?" her question was little more than a whisper.

"You are mine, Tiger Lily. There will be no other women. I don't want other women."

I shook my head trying to get the words to come out right. But all I could see was her naked flesh, glistening with the passion I had already given her.

I loomed over her and gently bit her neck, "And you will have no other man. I will be the only one that touches you, fills you, and completes you."

"Yes," she moaned long and loud, as my finger sank into her hot core.

Lily was impossibly tight, her virginal walls clamping down on my fingers in a vice-like pull.

"You are fucking tight, Little Princess!"

She mewled as I added another finger. I loved watching my fingers become coated with her heat.

Lifting my hand, I licked them, and her eyes widened.

"Do you want to know what you taste like?" I rasped, placing one finger against her lips.

She sucked it inside of her mouth and swirled her tongue innocently. My cock throbbed in my pants thinking about those pouty lips wrapped around it.

"Fuck, Lily, that feels good!"

Her cheeks heated, and she let my finger go with a pop. I took off the remainder of my clothes as her heated stare never left my body. I knew that my cock was large, but the look of trepidation in her eyes had my lips twitching.

"This isn't going to work," she said nervously.

I didn't answer her, only walked up to the berth, and pulled her to the edge. Spreading her thighs once again, I stroked her pink folds with the round head of my dick. Lily's eyes widened and then rolled back as her pussy began to throb with need.

"Hands above your head, Princess," I growled out a sound of approval as her small tits thrust into the air like an offering.

It was one that I was more than willing to partake in. I sucked the small brown nipple into my mouth, still stroking her pussy. I knew that she was trying to hold still, but she strained against my lips. Arching her back and trying to shove her flesh further into my mouth.

I smiled and moved to the other nipple teasing and flicking it in rhythm to my cock.

She cried out as her release washed over her, and I felt the juices of her heat. It was now or never. I sank into her and then stilled as her body adjusted to my size.

"Too big!" she panted, "You are too big!"

There isn't a man alive that doesn't want to hear those words. If they tell you differently, they are working with a pencil penis or lying.

But I didn't want to hurt her.

"Just relax, Lily," my voice sounded like I had been swallowing glass.

I leaned down and kissed her, ignoring the throbbing of my dick. I had to make this good for her, because the Lord knew that I had never had better.

Her tongue shyly came out to play with mine, and I felt satisfaction in my gut. Her legs eased open a fraction more, and I sank in a little deeper. She didn't seem to notice as I kissed the shit out of her.

I could spend days just kissing this woman. Every nuance of her was exciting and fresh to me.

She rocked her hips against mine, whether involuntary or not, it was my invitation to move.

I pulled out slightly, and she whimpered, "Don't leave."

Fuck me.

If she hadn't already stolen my heart, she would have ripped it out with that whispered plea against my lips.

"Never," I slid back inside, and her eyes opened as a low groan escaped her lips. I moved back and forth inside of her tight sheath.

Sweat began to pour down my back. I had never fought so hard to keep from coming. But I wouldn't come until she did.

My strokes increased, and her moans deepened. She was so wet that I heard a squelching sound with every pump of my hips.

I picked up her ass and tilted her upward so that I could reach deeper, fill her further.

Lily's hands gripped my shoulders, her nails digging into my skin. I felt her pussy clench around me with every slide of my cock.

I couldn't keep up the slow pace. My body demanded hard and fast. With a growl, I began to thrust in earnest. Fucking her tight body as it needed to be fucked. Lily blossomed underneath me. Her hands moved to my back and clawed out her approval.

Her cries consisted of my name and all the Gods rolled into one. I knew she was close, just as I knew that I was on the brink.

"Cum, Lily, Cum," I demanded with a final thrust that sent her eyes rolling back, and her hips shaking in my hands.

Her orgasm swept through both of us as her pussy contracted repeatedly on my cock. I filled her with ropes of cum that seemed to be never-ending. I had never come so long or so hard in my life.

I couldn't move, could barely breathe as I propped myself on my elbows. Her eyes were shut, and her breath was coming in pants.

"Lily," I whispered, kissing the corner of her mouth.

Her dark eyes flickered open, and she arched a thin brow, "You are mine, Alex. There will be no others."

I tried to hide the joy that her possessiveness brought out in me.

"And that is your command, Little Princess?"

She flushed, and I became acutely aware of her diamond hard tits against my chest.

"That is my command," she said regally.

I kissed her eyelids, then her cheekbones and chin, finally I came to her mouth and kissed it softly.

"Then it shall be so," my vow soaking into both of us.

Her lips trembled and then a shy smile broke out.

I felt myself softening and pulled my cock from her warmth. Her eyes showed immediate disappointment, and I knew that I would never get used to her beauty. Not if we lived another thousand years or more.

I turned to walk to a basin to grab a rag, and she cried out in horror.

"Your back! Did I do that? Goddess, Alex, I am so sorry!"

I wanted to tease her. She looked mortified. So, I didn't.

"Badges of honor, Little Princess. You marked me as yours just as surely as I marked you as mine."

Her flush deepened, "I drew blood a few times."

My eyes darkened, "Perhaps I will feel it tomorrow, and it will remind me of the wildcat that I adore. I imagine that every time you sit, you will be reminded of me."

I ignored her gasp of surprise as I gently cleaned her pussy before throwing the cloth to the floor and gathering her into my arms.

Her contented sigh, as she nestled into my chest, would be one that I will cherish for the rest of my days.

36

TIGER LILY

"My queen," Silver's silky voice was in stark contrast to his eyepatch, peg leg, persona. "We need to get to the bottom of the bay. Surely, we can come to some sort of compromise?"

The mermaid queen eyed the old pirate warily. Mermaids were notoriously vain and effortlessly sensual. Besides Silver's voice, there was nothing about him that a mermaid would want to take a second look at.

"I have been swimming these waters all of my life, Captain," the queen shook her dark hair, and one of her small dusky nipples peeked through her hair.

My eyes immediately went to Alex's. I told myself that if he was looking it was only natural. That guys were attracted to naked women. It didn't mean anything. He wasn't acting on it.

But in my heart, I knew that if he was staring, I might have to remove his balls forcefully.

To my surprise, he was neither looking at the queen's exposed breast nor her face. Alex was staring straight at me with a small knowing smile on his lips.

Sure, I was a little insecure about my breasts. There was nothing wrong with them, but they weren't huge like Ebony's. And I didn't flash them about as the mermaids did.

I lifted my chin and raised a brow in silent question.

Alex's lips lifted higher, and his eyes began to dance.

Damn him and his knowing glances! And damn this stupid green-eyed jealousy that was threatening to eat me alive.

I scoffed and turned back to Silver and the mermaid queen who were now arguing terms. There seemed to be some disagreement about Silver's bribe, he had brought along gold, and while the mermaids enjoyed pretty things, I knew immediately that it wasn't going to sway them.

My insides were at war. I didn't know if helping Silver to try and out trick him later had been the best idea. But that was the situation I had found myself in.

"Do you have jewels, Captain Silver?" I interrupted him mid-sentence. "Do you have fancy looking glasses, tiaras, necklaces, and rings?"

The mermaid queen immediately sparkled, "Yes, bring all of that and more, and we will allow you to explore our bay."

Silver's eyes narrowed at me, and I smiled innocently back at him.

"Tiger Lily," he barked out, "If you will assist me?"

I knew Alex wanted to grip my wrist. He didn't want me alone with Silver any more than I wanted to go. But I followed him anyway, because if we were going to do this, we needed to do it right.

Once we moved off from the group Silver turned to me, "Just what sort of game are you playing lassie?"

I gulped but held his gaze, "The mermaids think they are the most beautiful creatures alive. They have no use for gold. But anything that they perceive to enhance their beauty will be of worth to them."

Silver got an odd glint in his eye, "Would they know the difference between glass and the real thing?"

He was starting to catch on.

"No, Captain, I don't believe so. They are concerned about the appearance of something, not the quality."

The old pirate's wicked grin was infectious.

"Well then, lassie, I have just the *treasure* for this fine merfolk."

He signaled to his first mate, and they had a word in private. It wasn't more than fifteen minutes later that Black Dog returned with a small chest. Upon opening it, Silver showed the mermaid queen several shiny necklaces and sparkly tiaras. I would imagine that they would have been popular at an earth girl's birthday party.

But the mermaids didn't know that.

Draping themselves in the jewelry, the mermaids sat admiring themselves and each other in the small handheld mirror that Silver had taken from his own cabin.

There was a rustle among the crew that he certainly never used it. I politely refrained from commenting.

Alex's mouth hung open as we strapped ourselves into the diving gear.

"How did you know what to do?" he asked in a low voice.

"It's about knowing your audience," I said loftily.

His eyes widened before a small smile broke across his whiskered jaw.

Damn, he was sexy.

"What would you have offered if I was the mermaid queen?" he asked, thinking that he would have me stumped. "I am not partial to jewels, and I have plenty of gold."

I scoffed, "That is easy, you should really have given me a hard one."

His eyes narrowed, "Go on then, what would you have offered me?"

Right as he stuck his mouthpiece up to his lips, I pushed him back into the water. But not before answering, "Me."

I saw the look of surprise and lust cloud his features before he sank into the depths. Attaching my mouthpiece, I quickly followed him. The Mermaid Lagoon was clear and had tropical fish that mingled with the coral reefs, that lived just below the surface.

I was surprised to see so many mermaids. There had to be at least twenty. But we weren't there for the mermaids. We were there for the map.

Alex and I swam out a little further, until we were close to where some of the old shipwrecks littered the bay. We searched up and down every one of them. It seemed like we had been down there for hours, but it couldn't have been that long. We didn't have enough air in the tanks.

Sadly, we had gone through every ship, and not one of them held the map.

Just as Alex was signaling that we needed to go up, I saw a strange looking piece of coral that didn't look natural. I waved Alex off and swam over to the reef. This area was blackened and seemed incongruent with the rest of the area.

I grasped the long piece sticking out, but nothing happened. It had been a long shot, but I figured it was worth a try. Alex was swimming over to where I was and indicating that we had to leave.

I knew that, but I also had the strangest feeling that something wasn't right. I looked around and saw the queen eying us with hatred. Her teeth were sharpening to little points.

My hand went back to the coral, and I twisted, pulled, poked, and prayed. Because with a shrill cry the mermaid queen pointed to where we were swimming. Alex didn't hesitate to yank three times on our ropes. That was the indication that something was wrong. I felt the jerk as the pirates began to pull us up.

I didn't want to give up!

Frantically I moved my hands over the coral as I felt my body begin to lift. At the last minute, I punched it with everything that I had, and it shattered. Alex looked at me in surprise, as a tube popped up out of the coral.

I grabbed it with the tips of my fingers just as we were yanked closer to the surface. The merfolk was racing towards us, but they hadn't been close enough, to begin with.

The second we cleared the water. Alex ripped his mouthpiece off.

"They are coming, hurry!"

We were pulled unceremoniously onto the deck of the ship, just as the merfolk broke the surface.

The queen was shouting obscenities, but Silver would hear none of it. A deal, after all, was a deal.

The mermaids closest to the ship threw their jewelry at the ship. But most had terrible aim, and it began to sink into the water. With a scream of outrage, they began to fight amongst themselves as other mermaids stole the tossed goods.

Silver wasn't stupid enough to hang around. As soon as the wind hit our sails, we left with the map in hand.

37

ALEX

"What in the hell is this?" Silver raged as we all stared at the blank map. Obviously, it had been created to work in code, but without the knowledge of how to release the images, it was about as useful to us as toilet paper.

Silver tried using smoke, almost damn near burned the sheet up in the process. He tried salt water, sand, and even blood. But no matter what he tried, nothing worked.

Tiger Lily was once again locked up in the cabin below, and I was glad that she wasn't there to see Silver losing his shit. The man was ranting and raving at everyone. He sounded more like the red queen threatening his men that they were going to lose their heads, than the Silver we knew.

To me, there was only one person left to turn to, Tinkerbell.

If it was magic causing the map to be blank, she would be able to unlock it. I supposed that Puck could also help, but I didn't know about Peter. When he was tossed from fairy-land his magic was taken away. For a time, when he first came, Peter could still fly. But that had been a long time ago.

"We need the fairy, Silver," he flinched, as I voiced my opinion.

"We don't need any more fucking fairies, Alex!"

"Captain, if this is coded by magic, that is the only way to unlock it," I leaned in close. "And if Hook gets a hold of the map you might as well give up."

"Do you trust her? I haven't met a fairy yet that is worth putting my trust in. Shit, the reason we are in this mess is that Peter stole the treasure from me in the first place, and then Hook got ahold of it. I wish I knew what happened to it after that."

It struck me at that moment that I didn't have a fucking clue what I was doing. I was double-crossing Silver every bit as much as Peter had all those years ago. To make matters worse, I was working for my father who didn't have the decency to claim me as his bastard son.

Was I fighting on the right side?

Who were the good guys?

Silver wasn't evil. He might be shrewd, double-crossing, and a downright dirty fighter. But did that make someone bad?

In the same regard, what was Hook? There had been times in my life when I would have sworn that he was the evilest man alive. But that wasn't true either.

"Why do you want the treasure?" I blurted out, not answering his previous question.

Silver's jaw ticked, "It's my treasure."

I got that. I really did. But something still nagged at the back of my mind.

"If you take it from Neverland, the island will die, all of these creatures will die. Are you ready to sentence everyone to death?"

Silver's jaw tightened, "The treasure doesn't make the island survive, it is the Never Stone."

"Isn't that part of the treasure?" I didn't understand.

It seemed like everyone was speaking in circles. Who was to be trusted or was anyone? I was starting to wonder.

Silver grunted, "I asked you a question before."

I raised a brow, "No, I wouldn't trust any of them." And then I looked him straight in the eye, "But I don't think I'd trust you either."

Instead of becoming angry, Captain Silver threw his head back and laughed.

"Smart Lad!"

I grumbled something about needing to check on the hostage and slipped down below.

As soon as I opened the door, Tiger Lily looked up from where she was reading on the berth. Her gorgeous eyes raked my face, and I felt my cock twinge.

Damn, she was so beautiful that it hurt to gaze upon her perfect features. I locked the door behind me and went to speak with her. But first I needed a small taste of her lips.

Tiger Lily tilted her head up as if it were the most natural thing in the world. The moment our lips touched I would have sworn that the room was illuminated with light.

Magic, this woman's love was pure magic.

And then I heard the voices.

"What the fuck?" I reluctantly wrenched my lips away.

Tinkerbell and Puck stood in the small cabin with bright eyes.

"You can't be here! Silver wants to capture one of the fairies to figure out the map."

"Why are you here?" Puck demanded, shoving Tinkerbell behind him. "I thought you worked for your father?"

"He might share my blood, but Hook has never been a father to me. Don't refer to that bastard as my father."

Tinkerbell raised her brow, and pushed past Puck, "Alex, what is going on?"

It didn't take very long to catch them up as to what was happening onboard the Henrietta. They filled us in on the camp of rebels.

"We went to Hook first," Tinkerbell added, "But he smugly said that he already had a plan in place. That must be you."

I felt like I had to lay out my misgivings, "I don't know who to believe."

Puck smiled, "You are smarter than you look, pretty boy."

I scowled as the girls giggled.

"Neither pirate should get a hold of the Never Stone," Tiger Lily wrinkled her brow, "The question is how we get it before they do and who do we entrust with such a valuable object."

"I have an idea about that."

I was shocked to see my best friend, Ebony, and Peter.

"How? What?"

Ebony raised one sassy brow, "Did you think that we would abandon you, Alex?"

"No, but I don't know how this is possible."

Ebony looked over at Peter, the love in her gaze, was almost embarrassing to behold. But I was happy for her. This woman had been like a sister to me all these years, and if anyone deserved a happily ever after, she did.

Peter cleared his throat, "Puck and Tinkerbell can be rather convincing when they want to be."

"So, what is the plan?" Tiger Lily asked.

Puck grinned and shimmered into the exact replica of Captain James Bartholomew Hook. Every affectation was the same from the way he held his head to the cock jut of his jaw.

Then Tinkerbell turned to Ebony, "It's time."

Ebony smiled at the curvy blonde, "Tinkerbell, I wish you were small again."

There was a flash of disappointment as the fairy began to shrink in size. I knew that she hated being in that diminutive form. But they clearly had thought this out, so I waited to hear what the plan would be.

Puck turned to the rest of us, "I should probably say that I am sorry for this."

His cocky smirk had me hesitant.

"What are you…?"

In a flash, we were all shrinking the same way that Tinkerbell just had. I watched Tiger Lily's hair lighten and her form change.

He wouldn't.

Shit on a stick—he did.

Fuck me if there weren't five tiny identical fairies gaping at each other.

"You made me into a fucking chick?" I fumed.

Puck's laugh made me want to put a fist through him. But considering that he was huge, and I looked like a firefly I resorted to flipping him off.

Tinkerbell smirked, "You even have the attitude down."

I wasn't even sure if it was Tinkerbell that had spoken. That smart remark had Ebony written all over it.

Then I looked down and realized I had tits. I know how inappropriate the thought was.

But I am a guy, and these things are like the holy grail.

I cupped my breasts, "Holy Fuck!"

Three very angry Tinkerbell's descended upon me, kicking my ass.

All the while Puck laughed.

38

EBONY

Then it was that there came into my head the first of the mad notions that contributed so much to save our lives.

-Robert Lewis Stevenson, Treasure Island

I loved Alex, but he could be the biggest douche. Tiger Lily wasn't speaking to him, and Tinkerbell kept calling him the pervert.

I looked over to where I hoped Peter was standing. It was hard to tell with five small fairies that were identical in size and appearance.

"Peter?" I called out in Tinkerbell's voice. The replica across from me nodded and I grabbed a string to tie around his wrist. "We need to be able to tell each other apart. I will pull my hair into a bun and use this sting as a bracelet on Peter."

Another Tinkerbell nodded, "I will put my hair in braids."

Obviously, that was Tiger Lily, so I looked at the last two.

"Alex wanted to wear this flower in his hair. Don't you pervert?" Tinkerbell lifted a white daisy and smiled.

Alex frowned with Tinkerbell's pouty lips, "I'm a dude. Why should I wear the flower?"

Tinkerbell scowled, "You are borrowing my face, pervert. You can do whatever I tell you to."

Puck laughed at her antics and looked on in adoration. I could only imagine what kind of trouble Tinkerbell and Puck got up to when left unattended.

After I finished tying the string around Peter's wrist. I was happy to see that I could tell the difference now between all the Tink's.

Peter had his string bracelet. Tiger Lily was in braids. I had my hair in a bun, and a surly Alex had a big white daisy in his hair.

Tinkerbell, the original one, looked the same as she always had when in her diminutive form. We looked to Puck, who was the leader of this madness, and he immediately went to the cabin door and flung it open.

Puck was still wearing the Hook glamor so there were automatic shouts from the pirates that Hook was aboard. The five of us, having been fairly doused in pixie dust, flew out of the cabin, and spread out to search for the map.

I had to hand it to Puck, it was a brave man who would take on a ship full of pirates by himself. But he had only scoffed and said it was child's play. I wondered how much of his confidence came from his magic? It didn't honestly matter to me as long as we found the bloody map.

I heard the clashing of steel and knew that swords had been drawn. With a small dagger in my belt I flew to the Captain's quarters where my natural father Silver might have taken the map.

It was much harder to search for something when you were gnat sized. I suddenly had a great appreciation for Tinkerbell and understood why she loved being life-sized. I had vowed to her that as soon as she wanted I would wish her big again. I never thought the day would come that I would count the woman as a friend.

But she had become more than a friend. These crazy vagabond warriors that had banded together, were my family. They had my back and I would gladly have theirs.

Taking one more look around the room, I decided that it wasn't here. Silver had to have the map on his person. He was undoubtedly in the middle of the fray with Puck. I flew out of the door and up the stairs.

The sight that I beheld had my stomach clenching. Blood ran along the decks of the Henrietta. Men were staring into nothingness, their necks—broken, their bodies lay in awkward angels that screamed of death. I could smell the acrid scent of metal in the air and knew that this would be a day I wouldn't soon forget.

Flying at top speed I raced to where Puck and Silver were sparring. Puck had a few cuts on his shoulder and one long slice across his face. I hoped they weren't deep, just as much as I prayed that this hadn't been a mistake after all.

Peter was flying around with his dagger slitting throats before the pirates could beat him away. I pulled mine from its sheath and followed his lead.

Taking a man's life was at once horrifying and satisfying. It is hard to explain the tumultuous feelings. But I knew that every man slain was one that wouldn't be putting a blade into my back or worse, Peter's.

I didn't see the flat of the metal before it smacked me down. My body shuddered under the impact. I wasn't sliced, but my head felt as if it were split in two.

I felt my forehead and my hand come away bloody. I was captured in the hands of Black Dog and he was marching me over to where Tiger Lily was already trapped in a cage.

I tried to fight, but my head made it difficult to think, much less reason.

I was dumped inside, and Lily immediately came to my aid. She pulled off a strip of fabric from our already tiny skirt and wrapped it tightly around my head.

"Ebony, are you alright?"

I wanted to assure her that I was, but honestly, I wasn't sure.

"My head hurts," I rasped.

Her worried eyes gazed down at me, "You are going to be fine. Do you hear me?"

I wanted to smile at her insistence. That was Tiger Lily to the core. Always looking for the better in a situation, always finding the silver lining.

The cage was opened, and Tinkerbell was tossed inside.

"Fucking asshole!" She had a gash on her leg that looked nasty. But she continued to flip off Mad Dog who was stalking away from where we were trapped in the cage.

"Holy shit, Ebony, are you alright?" Tinkerbell dropped to my side.

"Lil just asked me the same thing," I grunted. "I will live."

Tinkerbell looked at me dubiously, but Lily was already ripping another strip from her skirt to fix around Tinkerbell's gash.

She had little more than a belt now with the two strips pulled away. Her green panties fully exposed.

"Did you see Peter?" I gasped.

Tinkerbell nodded, "Puck changed him into another Hook and he is fighting."

"What about Alex?" Lily asked quietly.

Tinkerbell sadly shook her head, "I'm sorry doll. I haven't seen him."

We huddled together, trying to figure out a plan, and not vomiting every time we heard a man cry out his last breath.

I felt sick with worry and my head was throbbing.

Suddenly, the cage was being lifted, and we were sliding around the unsteady surface.

Black Dog had us.

He walked over to the deck where Puck had his sword jutting into Silver's neck. Peter was still fighting the last two men standing.

Black Dog shook the cage and I screamed. The pain in my head was too intense to handle such rough treatment.

There was a rustling behind us and then to my surprise I saw the end of a sword jutting out between Black Dog's pectorals.

Alex caught the cage before we crashed to the ground. He too was wearing a Hook glamor, but he was the only Hook I had ever seen with a large white daisy tucked into his black curls.

With the broad side of his sword, Peter slew the last of the pirates remaining. Corpses and carnage littered the decks of the Henrietta.

"You have lost, Silver," Puck growled out. "We have your ship; your men are dead, and I even have your daughter."

He flicked his wrist and all the glamor faded away. The cage we had been trapped in vanished and I found myself in my own clothes with a green strip of fabric keeping the gash on my head closed.

"Where is the map?" Puck demanded.

"I will never tell," Silver's eyes held more than a hint of emotion in them. But I couldn't tell if he was sad, or just angry he had been bested.

"We will kill your daughter," Puck bluffed.

I took a step back anyway. He was one scary fucker when he was mad.

Silver looked at me and then motioned me closer.

I took a hesitant step forward.

"Closer, girl," he demanded as much as one can with a sword at his throat.

I moved within range, to see the man whose eyes were so like mine. I wanted to scream at him, tell him that he was throwing everything away. That we could still make things work. I didn't want him dead.

But what he said next killed every bit of hope I had ever harbored about having a relationship with the man.

"I don't give a fuck about you or anyone. Best you learn that, girl."

I didn't hesitate, didn't even think before grabbing a fallen sword and sticking it though his gut.

There was a gurgle of something and I saw blood trail from his lips.

Then he smiled, "That's my girl."

39

EBONY

With a numbness that had frozen every inch of my soul, I watched as the dead were heaved into the sea. I had shaken off any attempts at comfort that my friends had tried to give me.

I had no wish to speak with anyone or to hear their pity.

It's funny how the world keeps spinning even if you have stopped. I've heard so many say that they couldn't go on if this or that happened to them. But that is a lie. You do go on, and that's the hell of it.

Time and tide wait for no man, and certainly not for me.

I wasn't sure how long I stood on the deck. I had watched until the last body had sunk into the murky depths. Captain Silver's eyes still held that mocking glint to them even in death.

'That's my girl,' he had said after I had pushed a blade through his heart. But I wasn't his girl. I wasn't Hook's or anyone else's. I had spent my life trying to be something to Hook, and he never gave a flying fuck about me. Now I learn the same about my real father.

I couldn't say that I was sad. I supposed that would come later though. It was as if I were devoid of emotion. A machine that went through the routine without stopping to understand what or why.

I helped to gather the weapons of the fallen. We worked in silence, only every once and a while Puck calling out orders.

The map was nowhere to be found, even after Tinkerbell searched Captain Silver's corpse. Had it all been for naught? I couldn't help but wonder which side we were on, the good or the bad?

I'd heard that every time you kill a man it tears apart your soul.

That too, is a lie.

Every time you kill a man, a small part of his soul latches on to yours. You carry with you the image of their breathing coming to a halt. The smell of blood in the air, and the look of terror in their eyes, it will never leave you.

Some men shit themselves, a natural reaction, but one that the storybooks don't often talk about. Other men have a frozen look of surprise, as if they cannot quite believe that they are fallible.

I wasn't about to let this mission be in vain. For hours I searched for that blasted map. I ripped apart the Captain's Quarters once again. Then searched the bulkhead, the men's barracks, even the stocks. But nothing, I couldn't see it anywhere.

Night was coming on and searching by candlelight wasn't conducive to a thorough search.

I felt Peter touch my arm, but I shook him off. I didn't want to be like this, I wasn't sure why I was like this. I couldn't help myself.

Suddenly I felt strong arms wrap around my body, and I was thrown over a broad shoulder like a sack of wheat.

I snapped to the present, "Get your fucking hands off me!"

Peter didn't respond but he did tighten his hold on my legs.

"I mean it, Peter!"

He smacked my ass and continued to carry me below. He walked right into our old cabin and told Tinkerbell and Puck to get out. I didn't even want to think about what they could have been doing there.

"Go and use the Captain's quarters, I won't be taking Ebony there."

I pounded on his back, outrage filling my soul. I was so angry. I couldn't control the depth of my anger.

He put me down but didn't let me go.

"You bastard," I seethed, "How dare you humiliate me like that?"

Peter's handsome face quickly scanned mine. It was as if he were making a decision and I had just thrown down the deciding factor.

There was one chair in this room, bolted to the floor.

He grabbed my shoulders and lifted me inches off the floor until he was able to settle me on the chair.

Quickly he bound my hands behind my back and linked them with the chair back. I could have gotten up had I wished to, but the angle would be painful, and I couldn't get myself free.

I screamed every obscenity I knew at him. But Peter ignored me. He went over to the berth, and to my shock, began to change the linens. My world was falling apart, and he was worried about the laundry.

He stripped the bed and threw the soiled mass in the corner. Then searching the drawers, he found fresh linens and remade the bed.

I seethed watching the muscles in his back as he did the work that servants usually did.

He was meticulous in his movements. Then once finished he turned to me, the love and sorrow he had in his eyes would be my undoing. There wasn't pity, but empathy by the truck load. The Lord knew that I needed someone, especially when I couldn't recognize it myself.

I began to shake, and his eyes widened. In seconds I was untied and in his arms. He didn't speak. What words could be used in a time like this? He didn't pretend to know what I was feeling or not feeling. He didn't spout off platitudes that would likely piss me off.

Peter held me.

In that instant, the frozen silence that I had retreated to, shattered all around me. Great sobs racked my body, and he held me.

I was a mess of tears, snot and who knew what else, and he held me.

I raged against the injustice of it all, pounding on his chest, and he held me.

He held me as if I would slip through his fingers if he wasn't careful. His arms were strong and true. He tucked me under his chin so that I could sob into his neck and I clung to him. I was lost, but he was my beacon. If anyone could guide me home again, it would be Peter.

I don't know how long we stayed like that. Seconds, minutes, hours, honestly, I couldn't reason with something as basic as time. All I knew was that his arms were the only thing holding me together.

After I completely exhausted myself, he kissed my temple and whispered into my hair.

"Sleep, my love," and to my surprise, I slept.

***I wasn't sure when I awakened, the sun wasn't quite up yet, but I felt rested. Certainly, much better than the night before. My heart still ached for what could have been with Silver. But wrapped in the arms of my lover, I knew where home was, and that was with Peter.

He had given of himself selflessly, and not complained once. I winced as I saw the scratches on his neck that I knew I had given him.

His body was hard and hot beside me as he slept. I could still see the concern etched on his sleeping face and it made me love him even more. His cock as nestled against my belly, hard and insistent.

I smiled thinking that even in times of heartache he wanted me just as much as I wanted him.

Suddenly, I needed to feel loved, I needed to have him buried deep inside of me. I needed his body worshiping mine as I worshiped him. I knew that taking advantage of a sleeping man wasn't playing fair, but I was a pirate, and pirates never played fair.

I sank down and slid his briefs below his ball sack so that his massive cock was free. Then ever so gently I traced the tip with my tongue. He moaned long and loud in his sleep, moving to his back.

I glanced up to see if he had awakened but he hadn't. Smirking, I continued my assault. Lick after lick, his musky taste filling my mouth and I wanted more. I wanted his precum sliding down my throat. I wanted to suck his dick as far as I could go.

Throwing caution to the wind, I wrapped my lips around him and sucked.

40

PETER

I was awake the moment Ebony broke free from my arms and slid down my long frame. I almost said something to her, but I remembered the night before and her terrible pain.

Grief can cause people to do crazy things, and a part of me wanted to know just what she was up to. If she thought she could leave my bed without my knowledge, she was beyond misguided.

When her small hands slipped inside of my underwear, my eyes flashed open, and I saw her gazing intently at my cock. I am man enough to admit that I had one small moment of fear that she was going to do something dreadful.

Like I said, grief causes people to do crazy things. But what happened next made me glad I'd gone with my instincts. She licked the outer rim of my mushroomed head and then glanced up at me. I closed my eyes the second I saw her head tilt and prayed she would think I was still asleep.

I wanted to know how far my little enchantress would go. I was not disappointed in the least. Her mouth closed over the tip of my cock, and she sucked for all she was worth.

My hips shot off the bed as I cried out, "Fuck, Ebony, are you trying to kill me?"

She smiled around my dick, and I swear I grew harder just at the sight. With bedroom eyes, Ebony closed her lips around me again and played with my length. Sucking rhythmically back and forth, taking little bits at a time, until I was panting.

My fingers ached to sink into her hair, but this was her show, and I didn't want to take that from her. With a pop she allowed my dick to free itself from the heat of her mouth and she licked my length like it was the best popsicle she had ever tasted.

I wasn't sure what garbage I was muttering. Something about her mouth rivaling the gods and fuck this, holy shit that, it was mass of cursing and pleading that had her feeling confident and proud.

Ebony grasped the base of my cock and took the rest into her mouth again. Pulling up and twisting slightly she began to take my length further and further into her mouth. There was a tear, as I accidentally ripped the sheets, before giving up and sinking my fingers into her hair.

I held her head and guided myself until I smacked the back of her throat and she moaned loudly. The vibrations had me wanting to shoot my load before I even had the chance to taste her.

I wrenched her off my dick, her look of disappointment was so precious that I couldn't help kissing the fuck out of her until we were both spiraling out of control. I needed to taste her, I had to taste her.

So, I lifted her up and sat her small frame on my face, "Hold onto the headboard, Ebony."

She blushed, and I felt a fierce surge of possessiveness for the woman I love. And then I brought her hips to my face and began to lick her. Her juices were covering my face, coating my tongue, and spurring me on. The moans out of her lips had my cock aching, and the way she sensuously humped my face was something that I will never forget.

I could spend days eating this woman and planned to wake her every morning with my head between her thighs. She was the nectar that I craved for existence. Her thighs tightened around my head, and I grabbed her hips forcing her to really ride my face.

I knew that she was worried about smashing me, which was ridiculous. But after a little encouragement, she really got into it. I could taste the change as she came for me, it was thicker and sweeter than the clearer juices had been.

Not wanting to pause for a moment, I flipped her around so that she lay beneath me. With the tip of my cock, I traced her folds. My lips found hers, and I knew that she could taste herself all over me. It was so fucking sexy that I couldn't wait any longer.

I slid my cock inside of her tight sheath and moaned at the pure bliss that was Ebony.

My hands found her nipples, and I rubbed them with the palms of my hands feeling them bead up beneath my touch.

The moment they became hard little points I tugged on them and reared my hips back to thrust harder, faster. Her legs wrapped themselves around me, and I tugged and pulled on her nipples using her moans of excitement to gauge what she liked.

I showered her breasts with tiny bites and open mouth kisses to soothe the sting. Her body was clenching, but I didn't want it to end, not yet.

I pulled her up so that our chests were smashed together and then used my strength to lift and drop her on my cock. I impaled her as far as I could go, loving the way she clawed her nails down my back and screamed my name.

Turning her body so that her back was flush with my front, Ebony reached between us and sank back down on my dick.

I was hitting her sweet spot in this position. There was no way around it. I rammed into her repeatedly and felt when she began to shake. She was coming and coming hard. One hand on her breast and the other caressing her pussy where we were joined I fucked her until she couldn't take it any longer.

Her body convulsed around me, and her cum sprayed out across the bed. I had never imagined she would be a squirter. The sweet liquid came and came and came as Ebony cried out my name, helpless to the passion that had enveloped her body.

There wasn't anything that I could do to stop myself from flying over the abyss. Her pussy was squeezing me so tight, wringing every drop of cum from me.

I was starting to see spots in front of my eyes, as my seed sprayed her womb.

We slumped over onto the bed. I knew that I was too heavy for her, but I needed a moment to catch my breath.

Holy shit that had been life-changing...

I held Ebony to me, "I know that you think you are all alone, but Eb you are the reason I get up in the morning. I am terrified that every day will be our last. Your laughter, your smiles, your smart mouth and especially your big heart have become a part of me. You are not alone, Ebony. I will always be the one standing at your side."

She was silent for a moment, and I worried that I had said too much. Maybe I shouldn't have brought up her heartache. But she flipped over to face me with her eyes misty and her lips trembling.

"You will be my family?" she whispered hesitantly.

"Your family, your mate, your husband, your heart," I pledged to her as I kissed the worried knot in her brow.

She took a few deep breaths controlling her tears.

"Thank you, Peter," her voice was raspy, and I knew she was struggling. My brave, valiant girl had been through so much. "I love you."

I felt her love all the way down to the tips of my toes. And shit, if I didn't feel the exact same way.

"I love you," I kissed her lips gently, pulling back when I heard rustling about on the ship.

"We have a pirate to stop and a treasure to find."

I smiled at her words, "So, a pretty uneventful day?"

She reached up to cup my cheek, "I love you, Peter Gallagher."

Damn, if that wasn't the greatest statement I had ever heard.

It's too bad it was followed by Puck's comments from beyond the door.

"I fucking love your arse too, Peter. Now dry off your dick and let's get a move on."

Ebony's lips twitched, "I know I shouldn't like him. He really is horrible."

I felt my own traitorous smile, "He's my best mate, what can I say?"

41

PETER

By the time Ebony and I had made it out on deck, there were plenty of catcalls, and lewd comments from Puck and Alex. Tinkerbell smirked most of the time, but Tiger Lily simply rolled her eyes at the shenanigans.

We started to sail back toward Hook. Without the map, we needed another way to try and locate the treasure. So, we were going to lie out of our asses and say that everything we had done was for him.

By the time we arrived back at the Indian Village, there was great rejoicing. Bonfires with wild boar on a spike rotated to perfection. You could smell the pork filling the air with its sweet, meaty deliciousness. The tribe knew how to throw a feast and were going all out.

Tiger Lily refused to speak with her father, the Chief, who was now taking full credit for her involvement. He was prick, no doubt about it.

I wondered why the father's in our lives had to let us down so badly. I glanced over at Ebony and thought about my child growing in her belly.

I could never abandon her or the baby and didn't know what kind of idiot would do that sort of thing. Hook had two girls on his lap in various disarray. Occasionally he would reach up and grasp a breast or cup their sex. It wasn't alluring or even scintillating. The man was a bastard to behave that way in front of Ebony and the other women.

I had always known that Hook had few morals that he clung to. But for a long time, he had protected Ebony. It made me wonder why. Because if she wasn't his daughter, why did he care so much?

The question circled endlessly around my head. I couldn't help but wonder if she was tied to the map somehow. Tinkerbell couldn't unlock it, and neither could Puck. But maybe Ebony was the key?

It made the most sense to me, but without the actual map, we couldn't test the theory.

Tinkerbell was dancing with some of the Indian maidens around the fire. Their faces alight with laughter as the drums kept their beat. It was lovely, and yet slightly foreboding that we were breaking bread with the enemy.

I wondered how many of the tribe would follow Tiger Lily once they learned we planned on double-crossing Hook. Surely, there wasn't any love lost for the old pirate that had been a scourge in their side for years? But I couldn't help but wonder what would happen.

"Why the face?" Ebony smiled up at me while wrapping her arms around my waist.

"Just thinking," I replied, leaning down to kiss her forehead.

Ebony raised a brow, "Care to share your thoughts?"

I smiled wickedly, and she blushed. It was beyond adorable.

"Perhaps when we are alone," I murmured.

Ebony nodded slowly, and then began to pull me near the dancers. I was not meant to dance. My large frame was conducive to fighting and kicking ass, not tearing up the dance floor.

"I don't think that is a good idea."

Ebony's jaw dropped. "Don't you own multiple clubs in the human world?""

I nodded, "Yes."

"Don't they dance at these clubs of yours?" she persisted.

Ebony knew full well that they did. I remembered the first time I had met her at my club in New York.

Damn, life had certainly gone off track after that. I am so damn grateful that Hook sent her away. I couldn't imagine a world without her.

"Yes," I said slowly, "But that doesn't mean that I partake in said dancing."

Ebony got a sensuous glint in her eye. Standing in front of me, she raised her arms and began to dance. Her hips were shaking with the beat of the drum. She didn't break eye contact as she dipped and swayed that perfect ass. Her hands trailed over her torso, while her fingers traced the edge of her corset.

She was provocative and so fucking sexy. My cock hardened, and I couldn't look away. I knew that there were most likely other men watching her, and it pissed me off. So, I did the one thing that I swore I wouldn't do. I walked up to her and pressed my front to her back.

My arm wrapped around her waist and she ground that plump ass against my cock as she danced enough for the both of us.

This wasn't dancing. This was having sex fully dressed, with music as a strong element of enchantment. And no, it wasn't lost on me that I sold the same type of thing at my clubs.

But I had never truly experienced the magic of it all until Ebony.

Her head fell back on my shoulder, and she moaned as I rubbed my cock against her ass in rhythm to the beats around us. My arm remained around her ribcage, locking her against me and letting every fucking idiot in the vicinity know that she was mine.

We danced for what seemed to be forever. Until her movements slowed, and she rocked back and forth content, and happy in my arms.

I would dance with this woman any day, anytime, and she damn well knew it.

"A DECISION NEEDS to be made about Hook."

The six of us had gathered in our quarters on the Henrietta to discuss the situation. It had been a week, and the map still hadn't surfaced.

Hook was acting cagey and aggravated, which was strange when you consider his enemy had been vanquished or had he? Hook had taken possession of his ship again. I couldn't help but fear that we were missing something important.

"We searched for Jolly Roger," Puck shrugged, "I don't think the bastard has the map."

Tinkerbell nodded, "Hook scowled and raged at anyone and everyone the whole time we were there; under invisibility of course, but he's not happy with his crew."

Tiger Lily spoke up, "In retrospect, I have never seen my father happier. He was whistling at breakfast. My father has never been a cheerful man. I think we need to search his tent."

Puck lifted a brow, "Tink and I are game."

Ebony looked over at me, "I think it's our best option now."

I had to agree. All of our leads had dried up, it seemed, "Do it, Puck. Report back tonight your findings."

Tinkerbell wrinkled her brow, "I can't help but wonder what happened to the lost boys? We haven't heard much from them. You don't suppose that they could have anything to do with the map's disappearance?"

It was good question that deserved looking into.

"Ebony and I will check that out. Alex, you, and Tiger Lily go over the Henrietta one last time. By the time the sunsets this night we will have that blasted map."

Everyone nodded in agreement and separated.

Ebony and I rowed a boat to shore and borrowed horses from the tribe to ride out to Hangman's Tree where the Lost Boys lived.

I hated to think that Nate, Charlie, or Tom might have double tricked us.

42

EBONY

The moment I saw Charlie's face I knew that something was wrong.

"What?" I didn't even bother to form the question, because I knew that he was aware of why we were there.

"I'm sorry, Eb," he scuffed his big size thirteen boot into the dirt.

Shit.

Fucking shit.

"What did you do?" I asked again, taking a step forward.

"Hook said he would burn our house down, Eb. He knows where we live, and he has spies everywhere."

I felt my blood pounding in my ears. And I wanted to rip his throat out. Peter grabbed the back of my pants, and I felt him trying to hold me back.

"What the fuck did you do?" my voice sounded lethal.

Charlie swallowed, "Gave the map to Hook."

I launched myself at him and found that I was dangling in mid-air by the seat of my pants. I wasn't sure if I cursed more at Charlie or at Peter, but neither one seemed too scared.

Ass-hats.

"You had better go back inside," Peter cautioned Charlie, and he didn't think twice before following the advice.

Once he was gone, Peter turned me around to face him. The bastard was trying to suppress a smile.

"I'm mad at you," I grumbled.

His brow rose, "Oh, I know."

"You shouldn't have stopped me from ripping him a new asshole."

Peter had to wait a moment before replying.

"It wasn't the new 'asshole' that I was worried about. It was that you were going to stick your hand down his throat and pull out his fucking balls that had me thinking intervention was needed."

I didn't even blush, "Well, do you think there should be more 'little Charlie's' running around? I was offering a public service."

Peter gave up the fight and threw his head back emitting a loud bark of laughter.

I really wished that he wasn't so damn handsome when he laughed, or didn't laugh, or breathed. I was in a piss poor mood.

"Tinkerbell and Puck are going to search for Jolly Roger," Peter finally calmed down enough to speak again. "They will find the map. If anyone can he will. That bastard is the trickiest man alive. I swear to you, Eb. We can trust him."

I grumbled all the way back to the rowboat and then on the long way to the Henrietta. It didn't help that when we returned I heard Tiger Lily screaming something about, "More, baby, more!"

Peter looked over at me in surprise, and I felt a traitorous smile crept across my face.

"You can still throw your voice, right?" I whispered to Peter.

He nodded, "What is the plan?"

"An invasion I think, from Hook," I grinned, feeling the weight of the day slipping off my shoulders.

"Not the Indian Chief?" Peter wriggled his eyebrows.

And we both stifled giggles, "Perfect!"

Creeping on tiptoe we stealthily made our way closer to the lovers. When we were within spitting distance, trust me I had shielded my eyes, Peter spoke, but it was the Indian Chief's voice that came out.

"How dare you defile the princess Tiger Lily? I will have your head for this Smead!"

There was a scuffling on the deck, and it sounded like Tiger Lily may have been dropped in the process.

"You call that a man-sword?"

I was choking on my laughter. Who in the hell uses the term 'man-sword?'

"My wives have used thimbles that were larger!" Peter continued, and I glanced up to see Tiger Lily and Alex yanking their clothes on and looking wildly about.

"There are a few lads that like a pretty face, Smead. I shall give you to them! You are not fit to rule the tribe!"

The lads had Alex drawing his sword and thrusting Tiger Lily behind him. But they still couldn't see us from our hiding place.

"Show yourself, Chief," Alex demanded.

"Why?" Peter retorted loftily, "You were busy showing 'yourself' what need have you with my great cock?"

Tiger Lily blanched, and I burst into hysterical laughter.

"What the fuck? Ebony? That had better not be you!" Alex was livid.

I was suddenly reminded of all the pranks we used to play on one another. There was more than one time I had been locked in the privy. Or when I had fish guts in my water basin, that was fun to be sure.

I had tears streaming down my face, and he moved the crates and found where Peter and I were hiding. I didn't even try to hide, and my body just shook with merriment.

Alex had been my best friend and constant companion for years. I didn't feel sorry in the slightest for what we had done, but Tiger Lily didn't really deserve it.

She would have to take one for the team if she planned on making a life with Alex. Because we were family, not related by blood, but by choice.

Tiger Lily was bright red with embarrassment, but Alex was just pissed.

"How did the search go?" Peter asked in a calm voice knowing full well that they most likely hadn't looked anywhere but at the other one.

Alex had the decency to snap his mouth shut. He was caught, and he knew it.

I wiped a tear from my eye, "Well, brother from another mother! That was well deserved."

Alex's tense form began to relax, and a sheepish look crossed his face. Then he glanced back to Tiger Lily who was hiding behind him.

"Don't be mad, Lily," I said, still grinning from ear to ear. "The opportunity was too good not to pass up."

She poked her head out from behind Alex, "We are sorry we didn't search for the map. We were going to, honestly!"

"But Alex's man-sword got in the way?" I couldn't help the small ribbing.

Alex rolled his eyes, "I should have known that the Chief wouldn't have said something so idiotic. But you bloody well sounded just like him."

Peter took a bow, "It has been a long time since I have done that. Thank you for being good sportsmen."

Alex grumbled something about hoping Peter's man-sword shriveled up and fell off. But I didn't care. We needed something to revive our spirits. Now, we just needed Puck and Tinkerbell to find that map!

We fixed something to eat and pulled out some wine to pass the time. It wasn't like Silver needed it anymore.

43

PETER

Ebony was three sheets to the wind. Apparently, she liked to sing as she drank, and my sweet little pirate couldn't hold a tune in a bucket. The more she sang, the harder everyone laughed and the happier our little band of misfits seemed to be.

I couldn't help but marvel at the way she had bounced back again and again. She was betrayed by Hook, her crew, Long John Silver, and now the Lost Boys. Most people would be wallowing in self-pity or doubt, but besides a little grieving, Ebony was resilient.

I admired so many things about her. I would like to think that since meeting her, I have become a better man. I knew I wanted to be better, not only for her, which I did, but for me. But she seemed to breathe life into me, when I was just moving through the motions.

Her cup was getting low, and I moved to refill it with the bottle of wine closest to me. Ebony grinned and swiped the bottle out of my hands.

"A real pirate doesn't need a glass," she slurred, "and we all know I am the most real of the real pirates."

Alex and I shared a glance of amusement.

Tiger Lily tilted her head to the side in question, "What is a fake pirate?"

The little hiccup that followed the question was both endearing and hilarious.

A wide smile slashed across Eb's face, "You were fucking a fake pirate earlier on the deck, have you forgotten?"

Alex scowled as Ebony, and I burst into laughter. Tiger Lily looked like she wanted to join in, but patted Alex's knee instead.

"I am rather fond of your man-sword, Alex. Don't you listen to those meanies."

Alex rolled his eyes, "Neither one of you can hold your wine. But thank you, my love, all the same. I wonder where Tink and Puck are? It's been a hell of a long time since they left."

Eb burped. It was so unladylike that she looked around to see where it came from. I gathered her loose limbs and positioned her on my lap.

"You are going to fall into a puddle on the ground," I whispered in her ear.

She smiled sweetly up at me, "You wouldn't allow that to happen, you are Peter Pan. I have spent months chasing you clear across the universe and back."

I loved this woman.

"What do you intend to do with me, now that you have caught me," I murmured, as I began to leisurely kiss her neck.

Ebony sighed and tilted her head to give me better access. "I will keep you! You will be mine forever."

My heart thudded, "Deal." I smiled against her skin, and she sighed again. This time the sigh sounded sleepier than before.

"Sure, the moment my back is turned you have a drunken brawl."

I turned to see Puck and Tinkerbell striding toward us. I couldn't help the broad smile as I noticed clutched in Tink's hands was an old rolled up parchment.

"We needed to save the wine for ourselves," I said jovially, "I assume you were successful?"

Puck scoffed, "Please, it was child's play."

I would have believed him if it weren't for the knife wound on his arm.

"Looks you had a little trouble," Ebony sat up, sounding less drunk. "Are both of you, all right?"

Tinkerbell nodded and then snatched the wine bottle from Ebony's hands and took a long pull of the deep burgundy liquid. She wiped her mouth with the back of her hand and then offered the bottle to Puck who shook his head.

"It isn't more than a scratch," Puck answered, and indeed it didn't look deep.

"Was it Hook who did that?" Ebony asked, as she tried to focus her eyes on the bloody gash.

"No," Tinkerbell answered, "it was me."

All of us swung wide-eyed gazes at the little fairy.

But it was Puck who spoke, "It wasn't your fault that idiot lunged at you."

Tink blushed, "We were in our tiny forms zipping around the ship. If you fly fast enough, most will mistake you for a dragonfly. But someone opened a door right as we were in range and I fell to the ground."

Ebony frowned, "Now that you mention it, I can see a faint bruise on your jaw."

Tink nodded, "I ran right into it and would have been stepped on if it wasn't for Puck. He changed us both to life-sized in a second. At that moment, the pirate lunged with a dagger and barely missed my face. I kicked the pirate in the nuts and as he fell the blade flew out of his hand and sliced Puck on the way to the floor."

Puck glanced at his forearm, "It is merely bloody, not a big deal."

Tinkerbell's lips tightened, "I will be sewing it up as soon as it's cleaned."

Then grabbing his arm, she poured some of the wine over it. Puck winced, and I could see his mouth muttering something that suspiciously looked like *mother fucker.* But he didn't cry out. He was one tough son of a bitch.

From there, Tinkerbell grabbed the first aid kit and sewed up the small cut. Had we been only men in the crew I doubted that anyone would have bothered with it. I was honestly surprised that Puck was letting her fuss over him.

The patience he exhibited was so far from the old Puck we had once known, that I felt proud of him and how far he had come.

Tinkerbell had handed the map to Alex when she began her ministrations. Tiger Lily and Alex were studying the blank page. But since smoke, water, blood, and fire magic hadn't made the parchment give up its contents I didn't think that staring at it would do anything either.

I still felt strongly that Ebony was the key to it somehow. Reaching out my hand, Alex passed it over to us. I felt a surge of disappointment when Ebony touched it, and nothing happened. I had been so sure.

She looked at it front and back and shrugged, "Just a blank sheet, I don't know what he could have been thinking."

Alex reached back over to take the map and the second he touched it while Ebony was still holding the other end scrolls of ink began to appear on the aged parchment.

"Holy Crap on a cracker!" Ebony exclaimed and dropped her side in surprise. Everything vanished, and it went back to being blank.

"Grab that map, Ebony!" I wasn't sure which one of us shouted it, and when she picked up her corner, with Alex still holding his, the map began to appear again.

We watched in tense silence as the familiar features of Neverland seemed to appear as if an invisible artist were standing before us.

There was the Indian Camp where we had left Tiger Lily's father and her tribe. Hangman's Tree filled in with long twining branches, looking eerily similar to how it had when Eb and I visited Charlie.

Cannibal Cove was at the south end of the map. This was where Hook usually kept the Jolly Roger back in his glory days. Mermaid

Lagoon where the map had been stored all these years under the murky blue waves.

And finally, Skull Rock appeared on the furthest northeastern point. There were jagged rocks there that made for dangerous sailing. There was a reason that it was abandoned. Most that ventured there never came back.

I supposed that I should have known what the map would show. One doesn't hide the most important treasure in the easiest place to find. So, when the bloody red X appeared at the base of Skull Rock I swallowed hard before speaking.

"We can't take the ship," Ebony spoke up before I did.

"You can't dive there," Alex ground his teeth, "That is the only place on the island that has sharks. How in the hell are we supposed to get there? And if we make it, how do we survive?"

Puck shrugged, "We fly."

44

EBONY

Blurry images flashed through my mind as I remembered the previous evening. I wasn't sure how much alcohol we ended up consuming, but every ounce of it was threatening to make a repeat performance this morning.

Peter didn't open his eyes as he muttered, "If you plan on going another round, you will either need to take this one by yourself or give me a few minutes."

My cheek heated, "I haven't the slightest idea what you are talking about."

I frowned because my mouth felt like I'd slept with gym socks stuffed in it.

A low laugh came from the sleeping form beside me. "You are joking, right? I mean, you were insatiable. There was once against the door, another time on the chair and then twice in our berth."

"I fell off the chair. Good Lord!" I exclaimed, as a slow flush covered my cheeks.

More and more of the previous evening flitted across my mind. I had yanked his pants down exposing that beautiful ass before we had made it inside of the room. The second the door was closed I was cupping his balls and sinking to my knees.

I hadn't sucked his cock for more than a minute before I found myself shoved against the door and my clothes being stripped off. He was in me in seconds. The slight burn from the sudden invasion had made it even more amazing. My head had fallen back and cracked against the wood door, and he slammed into me repeatedly.

I wish I could say that I gave him time to rest, but right after we had reached completion, I had felt the need to have him close again. I always wanted to be with him. It made perfect sense when you are whiskey soused and singing like a banshee.

I remembered singing a bawdy tune about a barmaid that fucked all the men in the town and came back for the women in the second round. Good grief, there was a reason I didn't drink to excess.

When Peter had said that if I sang one more song he would take me over his knee, I started singing in my loudest voice. I told him that a spanking was just what this naughty pirate needed.

"How much do you remember of last night?" I asked tentatively.

Both eyes opened with that, and he smiled that sex on a stick smile that had my heart melting.

And then in a deep baritone, he began to sing, *"There once was a gal named Sal, who strangely adored her wooden dowel. With lust and with need she rode her trusty steed and never cared how loud she howled."*

I giggled, "That was a good one."

He smiled back at me, "Thank you, but I can't take credit for it. I think you and Alex co-wrote it during your rum phase."

I winced, "We had rum?"

He nodded, "When the wine ran out."

"Did I beg you for a spanking?" I asked hesitantly. My ass felt sore, and I wanted to know how bad I had acted.

He nodded again, "You were screaming about how naughty you were and how you needed to be punished. Puck pounded on the door and said that if I didn't tan your hide, he bloody well would."

Crap on a cracker.

This big man had taken me over his knee while he sat in the lone chair of our cabin. One solid smack after the other rained down, peppering my ass cheeks with stinging bites. It had been brilliantly arousing, and I had begged him to take me, fuck me, and spank me again.

"Remind me never to drink again," I muttered, as Peter grinned at my discomfort.

"Don't worry too much, my love. Everyone else was just as intoxicated as you were. There wasn't anyone who could say they were well behaved."

I grumbled something and got out of bed to sneak off to The Head to pee. My body rebelled the moment I was upright, and I fought to keep my stomach from flipping inside out. My head pounded and even my toenails hurt.

I hadn't the slightest idea what was going on with me, but I knew I needed some privacy.

Once I had used the bathroom, I came back feeling better with my teeth brushed, and my tangled hair pulled up into a messy bun. Peter was right where I had left him on the bed.

"You are getting old," I teased.

Peter's eyes had been on me the moment I had opened the door. He had a way of making me feel that I was the only woman alive that mattered. I am not going to lie and say it didn't feel incredible.

His eyes glinted, "Do you want me to rub your sore ass?"

Let's get one thing straight, Peter could touch any part of me at any time and it would always be a good idea.

I dropped the robe that I had wrapped around me to go to The Head. Then I climbed back in bed and turned my back to him. He pulled me close until my back was flush with his broad chest. Then he lifted my leg and moved it back a bit so that I was open to him.

His fingers began to softly stroke my folds. My eyes rolled back, and I bit my lip, and a low moan erupted from my lips.

He slipped a finger inside of me and pumped it in and out, having a second finger join the first. I panted with increased need as he scissored his fingers, grinding and rubbing my slit so well that I was on the cusp of coming.

"Peter," I panted his name, wanting him inside of me, around me, claiming me.

I felt the blunt head of his dick against my ass. He moved his hips back and forth so that his cock could brush gently against my pink skin. It felt beyond amazing, and I couldn't keep quiet. I moaned again as he fingered me to the rhythm of his thrusts.

When I was sure I couldn't take another moment, he slipped inside of me. Laying on our sides gave him the ability to go deep and stay there. Time and again he moved his hips back and forth, the wetness squelching between my thighs.

"Please, I begged," and Peter made sure to answer my cry.

He pumped his hips a little faster, making sure to read my body signals whether they say go fast or get the hell away from me. He knew just what to do.

I found myself hovering on the abyss once again. But Peter didn't want me to climb to the top and not see the view. It was seconds before he had his hand between my thighs and was rubbing. The fire in my belly increased a hundredfold.

I shattered, I flew over the cliff and dragged Peter along with me. I wondered if he had lost his ability to talk because for a while he just lay there panting.

"Good?" I asked cheekily.

"Bloody fantastic," Peter sputtered, "Damn woman, you never cease to surprise me."

I couldn't help the happiness that radiated off my face. I wasn't sure what the day would hold and if the map would even work. But I trusted this man, and I loved him.

Things would work out, they had to.

45

PETER

Flying had been the one thing that I missed the most about my lost past with the fae. Puck had said that since I was technically reinstated, I should have my magic back, but I couldn't find it within me.

I still had the dull ache, like a phantom limb that was missing. Over the many years, it had dulled, and I almost didn't notice it most of the time. But I was acutely aware of it in times like these.

Puck and Tink had sprinkled us all with pixie dust so that we could not only shrink in size but that we could fly to Skull Island. The camaraderie from the previous evening was still present. But it was a solemn affair as they took flight towards the deadly piece of rock.

Skull Island wasn't large, perhaps only a mile in width and two in depth. The old rocks vaguely resemble a man's skull hence the time. When I was a child running amuck as Peter Pan, we would sometimes play there.

That brought back memories that I wanted to forget. The last time we had been at Skull Island had ended in tragedy. I remember Stevie's little face, so dirty one could hardly tell the color of his skin, but those black obsidian eyes were expressive enough to sear themselves into my soul.

He had run off trying to prove that he was man enough to his fellow Lost Boys brothers. Some had teased him because he was a little smaller than most. His ribs stuck out of his ribcage no matter how much he ate.

I found myself remembering the funny things he would do. Like, insist on sleeping with the dogs even though he often smelled of piss and dirt. The way he would sneak into the Indian Camp and return with feathers and dried meat.

Stevie was fast, fierce, and stupid. He thought that he was invincible, but hadn't we all?

I wasn't sure if it was Cubby or Tootles that had kicked him out of the hut that night. He had rolled in dog dung, and it stunk to high heaven. Stevie wasn't about to take a bath; Lost Boys didn't bathe.

So, the guys booted him out to sleep under the stars. It wasn't like any one of us hadn't had that punishment before. Everyone, except me, that is. I felt a tremendous amount of guilt over what had happened that night.

Somehow Stevie had gotten a raft and sailed for the deathly Skull Island. Determined to show all of us that he was more of a man than we could ever be.

It was the mermaids who brought him home to us. You can't know what someone looks like who has drowned unless you've seen it. Nothing prepares you for the bluish tint of their skin from the lack of oxygen to the blood. Their body swells to the point where it is difficult to recognize the individual. Even their tongue swells, looking grotesquely large as it protrudes from the victim's body.

I swallowed hard not wanting to picture that sad scene any longer. I think a part of my childhood died that day. It wasn't long after that I left Neverland looking for something to distract my thoughts, and I ended up all the way on earth.

I still had enough magic to fly back then. But as I continued to age, the magic left me. I figured that the fairy had finally deemed me unworthy of it. But now I wondered if I had personally abandoned it.

Was it my sadness and grief that had pushed it away?

The thoughts continued to plague me as we flew across the water. In the morning light, the sun danced across the surface. It looked as if shimmering jewels glinted with the promise of treasure to come.

I couldn't give a fuck about the treasure, but suddenly saving Neverland had been imperative. I had to have more time with Ebony. I needed to secure the homes of my friends. I owed it to them for leaving all those years ago, especially for abandoning Tinkerbell.

She was a handful, and I am sad to admit, that I was thankful she was no longer my problem at the time. But I had been too young to realize that friends didn't do that to each other.

The island came into view, and we raced just above the water as we made our approach. I was determined that there wouldn't be another tragedy at this forsaken place.

We flew into one of the openings that resembled an eye. It was dark and smelled of mildew. You could feel the lack of current in the air as it weighed on our bodies even in this tiny form.

"Spread out," I commanded, "Look for a bright blue stone. It won't be large, perhaps the size of a man's clenched fist. But the color will be brilliant, and it will seem alive under the surface."

Everyone nodded and flew apart as we searched. The cavern felt as if life hadn't touched it in a hundred years or more. It wasn't hollow as one might have thought. But it contained hundreds of passageways that often intersected and at times came to a dead end.

The distance between the water and the roof of the tunnel was only a few feet. Not wide enough for a grown man to stand, but a space that one could swim in.

The tunnels weren't smooth either. The sides often had sharp spears that jutted out from the walls. Whoever had carved these, didn't want anyone to follow in their footsteps.

As far as a place for buried treasure, I had to admit that there was not a finer spot on Neverland. I just hoped that we lived through it to tell someone about it.

As we entered the heart of the island, we heard an eerie sound, almost like a woman weeping. Ebony looked at me in alarm.

I took her hand, knowing that asking her to stay behind was futile. As we dipped and turned through the maze of tunnels, a bright light appeared in the distance. Increasing our speed, we raced to see if perhaps we had discovered the Never Stone after all.

We had two more corners to turn when the tunnel broke open into a large cavern. It was beautiful in a stark sort of way. But that wasn't what had the hair on my arms and neck standing at attention.

In the center of the cavern locked in a cage was a woman. Her hair was white as snow, ratted and dirty, and it clumped around her naked shoulders and chest. Her eyes were the bluest color I had ever seen, much like labradorite. They glowed in her thin, pale face.

I knew the moment she looked at us who she was. By the harsh intake of Ebony's breath, she had realized something similar.

We flew closer, and the woman kept her eyes on us the entire time. Her mouth was still singing that achingly haunting sad song.

The features of this woman were so familiar to me. I almost had a hard time looking at her. Who would have done such a horrible thing?

We easily flew through the bars of the cage. Inside, we could see that she had a massive chain attached to her ankle. The moment our feet touched the ground she spoke.

"My Ebony, you have found me!"

The woman didn't look much older than Ebony, but her facial features were nearly identical. Ebony took no time approaching the much larger life-sized woman and reaching out to touch her as if she were not certain of the realness before her.

"Mother?" Ebony's choked reply, wrenched at my chest.

The woman's blue eyes swept over her daughter's tiny fairylike form with so much love and tenderness that I knew this woman wasn't evil.

It was at the second that Puck and Tink entered the cavern from another tunnel. They both gasped when they saw the woman. Flying into the cage beside us, Puck changed Ebony back to her life-sized form.

"I have waited many years for you, child," the woman's face held sadness, longing, and perhaps a glimmer of hope. "There isn't much time left."

"What do you mean?" Ebony took her mother's hands on her own. "We have just found you."

"My light is dimming, and it is time for me to pass this power onto you," the woman said kindly. "I have served as the Never Stone for many years. It is time for you to take my place."

46

PETER

"Like hell, she will!" I tried shoving Ebony out of the way, but she looked at my miniature self, and to my surprise, she laughed.

"You are adorable!"

I wasn't adorable. I was a fucking man for Hell's sake, and I wasn't about to have the woman I loved be chained and left in this cage.

So, I bit her. Not the Never Stone, Ebony's mother, but I bit Ebony's arm…. hard.

"What the hell?" she brushed me away looking at the tiny bite with confusion and irritation.

Puck changed us all to our human form. The Cage was about the size of a twelve by twelve room. So, we were all able to fit in, but it wasn't comfortable.

Alex smirked, "You offended his manhood, Eb."

Yes, she had, but I didn't need his help, nor was I about to admit it.

"Ebony will not be chained up in some fucking cave," I growled, "I will not allow it."

The Never Stone's eyes sparkled, "Peter Pan? You are all grown up now, aren't you?"

I had been for quite some time, but I didn't see this as a viable way to convince the woman she wasn't going to trade places with Ebony.

"I remember you coming here as a boy. You tried to help Stevie, and it was very brave of you."

I felt my throat tighten, "What do you know of Stevie?"

She looked at me, her eyes glowing and I saw his image clearly sketched in their depths.

"I tried to save him," she whispered, "I begged him to go back. But he was insistent. Stevie wanted to take back my eyes to show the Lost Boys that he was a man."

I felt bile in my throat, "So, you killed him?"

She paused, "No. But his greed killed him. He drowned after falling and hitting his head on a rock. I couldn't get to him."

As she looked at the long chain attached to her ankle, I realized how horrible it would be to watch a child die and not be able to help them.

"I am sorry I accused you."

"I know you think that I am the villain in this piece, but I am not," she went on to say. "I never wished to be the Never Stone."

Ebony took her mother's hand in her own, "How did it happen?"

"Your father had heard of a place where mermaids swam freely through the sea. He said that dreams came true there every day and so why not ours. We wanted a child. You see very badly. Or at least I wanted a child. I realize now that my husband, Silver, was after more than just my dreams. Once we landed, the island was a wasteland. There weren't any of the lovely things that he had spoken of."

The Never Stone smiled sadly, "We were about to leave, heartbroken when a great storm rose in the sky. We secured the ship as best we could and planned to see the storm out before leaving. I was secured below when I heard something. I wasn't sure if it was a baby cry or an injured animal. But I left the protection of our cabin."

"You sound like your daughter," I said gruffly, and Ebony gave me a look.

"I remember the sky was filled with lightning and the roar of the thunder always knocked me off my feet. It was a glorious display of God's talents, and I was completely captured by it. There was a bolt of lightning that I never saw coming. One moment I was on the deck of the ship and in the next, I was chained in this cage. My hair had turned white, and my eyes glowed blue."

She laughed bitterly. It was a sound that broke my heart.

"What happened?" I begged her to continue.

"It was a trap," the Never Stone said looking up, "Hook had conspired with a witch to disguise the island. He then lured Silver here with promises of fame and fortune. But the truth was that they needed another Never Stone. The current one was dying. What we didn't realize was that I was already expecting when I arrived. So, when the lightning struck me, it gave the power of the island to my child as well. At first, your father took you, but the battles between Hook and Silver were constant. It wasn't until Hook promised me that you would be raised with all the love and care that I couldn't give, that I helped him banish Silver. I had loved my husband, but he was willing to trade me for the things Hook had offered him. Of course, I knew Hook would never be a good father. But I couldn't feed you, and I wasn't about to let my child be raised in a cave."

"Then why would you want to trap her there now?" Peter demanded.

The Never Stone wrinkled her nose in confusion, "I have no wish to have Ebony live in this cage. But I needed her to break free from the chains. I am not powerful enough on my own. I have waited for this moment her entire life, when we can destroy Hook once and for all. My time as the Never Stone is running out. Our chance to get rid of him is slipping through our fingers."

"What do I need to do?" Ebony asked.

"You are just going to believe her?" my voice held more than a note of disbelief.

Ebony turned, "She is my mother. What would you do in my place? I won't leave her here to die or for Hook to capture. I won't allow her to live in this cage a moment longer."

I grasped Ebony and kissed her hard. I didn't care that her mother was inches away or that we were surrounded by friends in a rotting cave. I wanted her to know how much I loved her and that I was dying inside at the thought that something might happen to her.

"Can't Puck's magic break you free?" Tinkerbell asked.

The Never Stone shook her head, "No, it is old magic on these chains. I will need a few drops of our blood to make the spell."

Ebony ripped out her dagger and pierced her skin before handing it to her mother. They dripped their blood over the chain, then she began to chant. I wasn't sure what the words were that were spoken, but her eyes glowed brighter, and Ebony started to join with her mother.

The chains began to burn away where the blood had mixed, and the cuff on her ankle finally broke free.

"What is your name, milady?" Alex asked as Ebony helped her mother to her feet.

When Ebony turned her eyes were glowing that same shade of aquamarine blue that her mother's eyes did.

"This is Aria, my mother."

I took her hand and kissed the back of it and was followed by Puck and Alex. Once it was determined that Aria could fly, Puck changed us back into tiny fairies, and we traveled along the dark corridors. Careful to evade the jagged spears and deathly water below.

The moment we broke free into the sunlight, Aria began to fall behind. Her strength had depleted from her years in the cave. It was decided that instead of flying all the way to the ship, we would go to the shore and rest.

Alex got a fire going, and Puck and I went in search of food. It was then that I heard a whistling noise whip past my ear.

Looking around frantically I saw them, Hook, and his crew were barreling straight towards us with knives and arrows at the ready.

47

EBONY

There are moments in time that I will always remember. The second I saw my mother's face, when Peter told me he loved me, and when Long John Silver died; these are all etched in a special place in my memory.

But nothing could have prepared me for the battle that commenced. We were outnumbered and fighting men that I had known my entire life. Some of them were far more of a father to me, than Hook could ever dream of being.

They came at us with a war cry, their swords raised, knives in hand and bows pointed at our heads. I don't know what I was expecting. But as I pulled my sword from its sheath, I felt a pang, knowing in my heart that at the end of this battle too many people wouldn't be walking away.

I don't know if everyone fights in their head as I do. It hadn't come up in conversation before. The clanking of the swords and the screams of the fallen seemed to fade away as I focused on my goal, survival.

The worst thing you can do in a fight is panic. In sword fighting, it is imperative to relax so that you can act with speed, control, and mental clarity. The posture and balance are second nature as you strike the opponent. Use sliding steps, be quick, keep your weapon close to the body; these thoughts kept rolling through my head as I killed one after another.

I didn't focus on the blood spattering all around us, or the smell of shit as men and women met their fate at the end of a blade. Your first attack is often the most important one, so make it count. The eyes, temple, throat, heart, or kidneys are where I aimed, and my sword was true.

A clean thrust into the abdomen and then twisting horizontally will cause the intestines to spill bile into the main body. Cutting the carotid will cause them to bleed out within moments. In truth, if you stab someone enough times they will die regardless.

So, when I saw my mother take a saber to her stomach, I froze. It went against every rule I had ever been taught. I didn't see my own opponent until their blade was at my throat. In an instant, I was thrown into the present.

Tinkerbell had a large gash on her cheek and was helping Charlie fight off some of the Indian Tribe that had sided with Hook. I didn't know when the lost boys had arrived, but as I looked around I saw many of them fighting on our side.

"Don't move, or it will be your head!" Hook hissed.

I looked up at the man that I had called father my entire life. The man I had left Neverland for, because I thought he was dying.

"If you kill me, we all die," I said in a much calmer voice than I felt.

Hook's eyes narrowed, "Don't you think I don't know that? This is your fault. Ebony. I wanted you to be gone from here so that when I ended it all, you would be safe. I never thought you would find Pan. Shit, if I didn't know for certain you weren't my blood I would swear you were my daughter. Always fucking things up, just like her old man."

"You want to kill everyone?" I hadn't considered this before. "It's not about the treasure?"

"There is no fucking treasure. I locked your mother in that cage eons ago. I thought I was being so clever, but like a complete idiot, I had to make a map. Sure, it was disguised, and difficult to read, but you figured it out. Damn it, Ebony, if I knew that I could get you off this fucking island before it dies, I would do it. I am not a good man, but I never wanted to harm you."

The lump in my throat felt impossible to swallow. I knew that my eyes were filled with tears. I had never heard this man say that he cared.

"Don't do this," I begged, "Please, you can't do this."

"I have to," Hook ground out, "Don't you see that? We are trapped here doing the same thing repeatedly. I won't leave your mother in that cage any longer, and I won't leave you vulnerable to men like myself and Silver. Besides, look around us, we have lost so many already. It is time."

"We can make things different," I sobbed, "Please, father, please."

I felt the bite of the blade against my neck and the sting as it sliced the first few layers of skin.

He looked at me with sorrow and regret, "Forgive me."

I closed my eyes and waited for the strike that would end my life. But it never came. I felt a jerk as the blade left my throat. I opened my eyes and turned to see Hook's lifeless body, with a blade through his head.

Peter was panting, his eyes wild, "Are you okay? Fuck, Ebony, I almost lost you!"

I couldn't stop the choked cries as he pulled me tight against him. The fighting was coming to a stop now that Hook was dead. It seemed that people weren't sure what to do. The dead lay around us in mangled forms, their blank stares etching themselves inside of my brain.

The cut on my neck wasn't deep enough to need stitches, I was lucky. But in the same respect, we had all lost a great deal, and each day after we would realize more and more the things that were lost in this battle.

A cry raised up above the crowd, "We are done with this useless fighting. Do you understand me?"

It was Tiger Lily. She had climbed on a rock and stood with the wind whipping her hair behind her. Her clothes were covered in muck and blood showing that she had been in the thick of it.

"You will pledge your allegiance to Ebony or die."

I knew what I had to do, "Stop!" I cried out. "I am not your leader. Princess Tiger Lily is the rightful ruler. You may choose to join her, or you will be given the same fate as those that have fallen."

One by one, they began to fall to their knees in front of Tiger Lily. She looked at me in surprise, but I nodded and made Peter release me, so that I too could bend my knee in allegiance.

Her father had fallen in the battle along with mine. My mother was in a very precarious place, hovering on the brink of death. It was decided that we would burn those that were lost.

I can't explain the silence that wrapped around each of us, and we watched friends, family, and enemies all go the way of the world.

Puck used his magic to stabilize my mother, but she was far from in the clear. His face as he turned to me, showed me that this man had truly done all that he could. It was the merfolk that eventually took her. They said they would have a greater chance of healing her, but that she would be tied to the waters from that point forward.

I stroked her long-tangled hair and cried against her chest. The wound had been closed with fairy magic, but her eyes hadn't opened.

In the end, I gave her to the sea with the hope that they could save her. But not before kissing her pale cheek and pleading that wherever she was, that she would find her way back to me.

Peter and I returned to the Henrietta, but the ship wasn't home. I had no desire to board the Jolly Roger and, so we gave it to Alex, because it should have been his inheritance in the first place.

The Lost Boys returned to their hut, in Hangman's Tree, and what was left of the Indian Camp returned to life, under Princess Tiger Lily's rule.

Peter and I stayed in Neverland, until we got news that my mother had finally returned to us.

I felt ill as we sailed for Mermaid Lagoon. Would my mother be angry at being trapped by the ocean? But the second I saw her. I knew it had been the right thing.

Splashing up onto a rock, my mother grinned at me. Her luminescent, bright blue eyes sparkled with love and life. Her white blonde hair fell on ringlets down to her waist. And her complexion was young and vibrant. She was beautiful.

I jumped into the water, not waiting for a boat and swam the distance to her. The sea couldn't hide our tears as mother and daughter were reunited again.

She kissed my face, "You were so brave, Ebony. I have never been prouder of you."

"I'm sorry," I sobbed, "I led you into danger, and you almost died."

"No, child," she said patiently, as she held me close. "You pleaded with a madman to save us all, and barely walked away with your life. You found a way to heal me. Never has there been a better daughter, I love you, Ebony."

I didn't know that I was waiting for the words, until I heard them. My mother loved me and was proud of me. I had been trying to please Hook my entire life, and always fell short. But all I had done was be myself, and my mother didn't ask for more.

I couldn't tell you how long we stayed that way. Peter and I stayed on in Neverland for several months getting to know my mother and helping to re-establish Neverland. It would never be the same, but there was hope and promise for a better tomorrow.

EPILOGUE

PETER

"The moment you doubt whether you can fly, you cease for ever to be able to do it."

-J.M. Barrie, Peter Pan

A piercing scream woke me from sleeping like the dead. I scrambled out of the berth and almost landed on my ass. I ignored the way Ebony snorted with laughter. I was trying to be the better person here, and it was my turn to deal with the monster.

Another wail sliced through the silence of the ship, making my ears want to bleed. When we first got the creature, I had scoffed at the naysayers who felt we weren't ready yet. For hell's sake, I was over a century old, how much more experience could I possibly need?

It takes a real man to admit when he was wrong. I am not quite there yet. But I will say that I was wholly unprepared for the chaos that has been our lives for the past eight months.

I gingerly made my way toward the screaming banshee, careful that when our gazes met, I didn't project trepidation or uncertainty. Creatures can smell fear from a mile away, and onboard the

Henrietta there wasn't any place I could hide, that the cries wouldn't find me.

The cage that we housed the creature had been bolted to the floor, the same as all furniture onboard. Just as I went to peek inside something was thrown directly at my head. But that wasn't the worst of it.

A smell, so foul and rank that it threatened to melt my eyebrows, wafted up and filled my nostrils.

I could do this. I looked inside and there peering up at me was the miniature tyrant that had ruled our every waking hour. She was smiling at me, and right then and there she once again stole my heart. Her curly brown hair was sweaty with sleep, and she had tear tracks down her tiny cheeks.

Her arms immediately shot out in the age-old sign of wanting to be held. And so, despite the fact that she smelled like a dead Kraken, I picked her up.

"What is your mother feeding you?" I blew raspberries in the chubby folds of her neck.

Her response was instantaneous. A riot of infectious giggles erupted from her, and I felt like I had just figured out world peace and solved world hunger in one shot.

I carried her over to the changing table, and with bravery and no small amount of gagging, changed her diaper. This was a testament to my commitment. The first time we faced off at the changing table she had squirted poo, the moment I was switching diapers. I had no idea that baby feces could be projectile.

"Is she hungry?" I heard Ebony sleepily call out from our bed.

"She's chewing on her fist," not sure how else to answer. The little monster couldn't talk back, and I hadn't figured out how to speak slobber yet.

"Would you get her pacifier? I think it's in her crib."

The Cage.

I wasn't overly fond of this contraption. It seemed to me like we were putting our daughter into prison every night. I had nightmares that she would trade those wooden slats for iron bars someday.

Did all fathers go through this? Did they feel as if their very lives are torn asunder by midnight feedings and baby powder?

I scooped her up as she batted at my face with her saliva coated hand. This didn't even bother me anymore. To think that the first time I had gone to a business meeting in New York with a baby thrown up down my back, unbeknownst to me, I dry heaved for thirty minutes.

"How is my favorite ladybug?" Ebony crooned as I handed her the offspring. I watched in awe as my gorgeous wife offered her breast to our infant.

Every time, every damn time, I had a tightening in my throat. I still had a hard time believing that this truly was my family. Ebony looked up at me in question.

"Is everything alright?"

I smiled down at them and then carefully joined them on the berth.

"Perfect," I replied. "We should reach Neverland by morning."

Ebony's eyes glittered with excitement. "I can't wait to see everyone. I wonder if Tinkerbell has had her baby yet?"

I shrugged, "It is their second one, maybe round two goes a little smoother? You just pop them out and keep going."

Her shoulders shook with amusement, "Thank you, Dr. Peter, for those words of wisdom."

I knew she was mocking me, "I do read those pussy parenting books you give me."

Ebony barked out a laugh, "Only when I take everything else out of the bathroom, and you are stuck with no other alternative."

"Our daughter is of much higher intelligence than the babies in those stupid books."

The moment I said it, the baby unlatched from Ebony's breast and smiled. It would have been perfect if she hadn't proceeded to scrunch her face and poop immediately after.

I had to back away for a moment. Her diapers were like a nuclear weapon. When I saw that Ebony was starting to rise, I shook my head and took the baby from her arms to go back to the changing table.

"Peter?" Ebony called out.

"Hmm?" I answered, not wanting to take my eyes off our daughter for a moment.

"I know that fatherhood hasn't been a walk in the park."

I frowned and finished changing the diaper before returning to the bed with the creature in tow.

"What are you talking about?"

Her eyes were kind, "I know you have had to make a lot of adjustments, and I appreciate just how far you have come. You no longer require plastic gloves to clean up vomit. I haven't seen you boil the pacifier for weeks. And as far as I know, you haven't been calling her 'creature' or the other favorite 'monster.'"

I gasped in mock outrage, "As if I would call my Katie-cat such terrible things!"

Katie giggled, kicking her arms and legs in the air. Okay, so I still called her creature and monster occasionally. I knew she wouldn't rat me out. First off, Katie has a pretty good gig here, and second, she can't talk.

But I didn't call our daughter creature because she was a terrible thing. Our little girl is the most beautiful little creature imaginable. I still marvel that Ebony and I were able to make something together that is so precious and utterly perfect.

In that same respect, not all monsters are bad, and this little monster loved terrorizing her father with the worst smells, stickiest hands, and wettest kisses imaginable. I loved every moment of it.

"Eb, I have never been happier in my entire life. You and Katie are my world. I didn't think I could love anyone as much as I love you, and now this little monster is in our lives, and my heart is so full it could burst."

Ebony sighed, "I am so glad you feel that way."

I nodded, "You know I do!"

"I just hope that you have a little room for one more person in that heart of yours."

I smiled, "I have all the room we need."

Silence.

Wait a minute.

Did she say what I think she said?

I gathered my girls into my arms with the largest smile a man could have.

"Are you sure?" I asked, tucking a strand of hair behind her ear.

Ebony nodded, "In the spring I think."

Placing my forehead on her own, I took a deep breath, loving the feel of my family around me and knowing that we had many adventures still to come.

"I love you, Ebony."

"I love you too, Peter."

Katie gurgled as she sucked on her toes, eyes intently on mine.

I gazed back, just as attentively at Katie, "I love you too, monster and your demon brother or sister."

"Peter!"

Katie and I laughed as the pillow crashed down on my head.

ALSO BY S. CINDERS

Adult Fairy Tale Retellings

The Dark Fairy Tales Series (An Adult Fairy Tale Retellings Box Set)

Scarecrow (Witch Queens: Tales from Oz)

Pan (Chasing Pan: Tales from Neverland)

Jabberwocky (Wicked Wonderland: Down the Rabbit Hole)

Goldie (Claiming Goldilocks: Tales from the Three Bears)

Regency Romance

The Dirty Bird Chronicles (A Regency Romance Box Set)

Maddie & CeCe Audio Book

Paranormal/Shifter Romance

Finn: Lycan Mating Games Book 1

James: Lycan Mating Games Book 2

Ella: Lycan Mating Games Book 3

Pavo: Dragon King's Series Book 1

Jord: Dragon King's Series Book 2

Promised: Wolves of Kencull (A Reverse Harem Shifter Romance)

Paranormal/Vampire Romance

Missing: A Virgin Vampire Ménage/Reverse Harem Series Book 1

Secrets: A Virgin Vampire Ménage/Reverse Harem Series Book 2

Hidden: A Virgin Vampire Ménage/Reverse Harem Series Book 3

Applebottom Magic (A Paranormal Romance)

Sci-Fi Romance

Becoming Super (An Urban Fantasy Sci-fi Romance)

Contemporary Romance

Special Delivery (The Billionaire's Secret Baby) Book 1

Special Recovery (The Billionaire's Secret Baby) Book 2

Royal Academy

Continue Reading for a sneak peek at Jabberwocky (Wicked Wonderland: Down the Rabbit Hole)

SNEAK PEEK AT JABBERWOCKY

"You can pack your shit and return to whatever hole you crawled out of, Harry! It will be a cold day in hell before I ever again involve myself in Wonderland politics."

Harrison was a shifter. Most residents of Wonderland could take on one shape or another. And for Harrison, well, he just happened to be a small white rabbit. It certainly wasn't as impressive as Cedric's Cheshire cat. Cedric could make different parts of his body disappear until he was only a floating pair of eyeballs or a sinister smile.

But at least he wasn't Darius who could only shift into a dodo bird—all body and no wings, tragic really.

However, what Harry secretly wanted to be more than anything was to be like Jay. Everyone wanted to be like Jay. He was a kick-ass Jabberwocky that owned his own freaking island and had chicks crawling all over him.

Chicks, meaning women, not to be confused with the poultry variety of chick.

Harry shook his head, "Al, you have to! The White King has declared war and the White Queen has taken to her rooms."

Alice raised a carefully crafted brow, "Explain to me why that is a bad thing? Perhaps they will kill everyone, just think of how great that would be?"

Harry's lips compressed into a thin line, "You know you don't mean that."

"I really do," Alice moved around her long-time friend Harry to pick up a few more plates that needed to be delivered at her small café, Treacle Tarts. "Look, I would love to help you."

"Why do I hear a giant butt coming?"

There was a snort of laughter from the kitchen followed by, "Maybe because you are speaking with my sister."

"Bite my ass, Lorina," Alice didn't even skip a beat, she dropped the lunches off, flicked her younger sister off and went to grab the coffee to refill some cups that she noticed were low.

Alice had opened Treacle Tarts as a way of supporting Lorina and herself. They were supposed to share the workload, but recently Lory had been slipping off frequently. And when she was there her work was only half-assed.

Every time Alice had tried to confront Lory, it ended up in a big screaming match between the sisters. They were as opposite in looks as they were in temperament. While Alice had dark hair, raven wing brows and a cupid's bow for a mouth. Lory was fair, with long blonde hair, peach stained cheeks, and a button nose.

One would almost think that they weren't related. That is until you saw the sisters around one another. They were eerily similar in many of their mannerisms, and their voices were almost identical.

"It would be a shame only to let me have a bite. With an ass that size we could feed half of Wonderland."

Lory came out of the kitchen with a hand on her slender hips.

Alice rolled her eyes, where Lory was tall and willowy, Alice was small and rounded. Her hourglass shape had caused no end of embarrassment for her. The men loved it, and the women hated her looking so damn good.

Alice knew that Lory meant no harm. The sisters had been trading insults from the moment they could talk.

"At least people want my ass." Alice turned to see Harry staring right at her posterior. She sighed before snapping in his face. "Was there anything else you needed?"

His face flushed as his eyes snapped back to her brown ones. He was happy to note that Alice wasn't angry. Harry knew that when Alice lost her temper, it was best to take cover and wait the storm out.

"Why don't you go ask Jay?" Lory interjected, having no shame in eavesdropping on the conversation between Harry and her sister.

"This is official business, Lory," Harry tried to put the blonde beauty in her place. "I am here as an emissary to the White Court."

Lory laughed, "Is that who you are serving now? Interesting that you made the switch. Didn't you used to be a faithful servant of the Queen of Hearts?"

Harry's face turned an ugly shade of puce, "That was a long time ago."

Lory shrugged an elegant shoulder, "Not so very long. I remember Alice having to go out and rescue Jay after you mistakenly had him imprisoned."

Her shit eating grin resembled that of the Cheshire Cat.

Harry narrowed his eyes, but it was Alice who spoke.

"Stop teasing him, Lory. It was ages ago. We were little more than children then. If Jay has forgiven him and let it go, we should too."

Lory just huffed and made her way back into the kitchen.

"I don't know why she doesn't like me," Harry muttered.

"Because you are a pretentious snob," Alice said with a smile, "And before you go getting offended by that. Remember, you are here asking me a favor."

Harry swallowed whatever retort had sprung to his lips. He hated when others were right. It was damned irritating.

"Look, Harry," Alice said kindly, "Lory might have been trying to yank your chain. But the idea is a sound one. Why don't you ask Jay to help you? He is a Jabberwocky for hell's sake. You can't get a better ally to have than a massive dragon that breathes fire."

Harry muttered something under his breath, but Alice couldn't hear him. She did note that he looked like he had been asked to suck on a dirty kitchen sponge.

"I did ask Jay," he finally relented, the words coming out like little knives.

"And?" Alice grabbed a rag and began to wipe down the pristine counter. Their café wasn't much, but she was proud of it and wanted it to show.

"He won't do it without you!" Harry spit out.

Alice's hand froze, the rag coming to a halt as she eyed the little red-haired man that sat twitching in front of her.

Images of Jay flashed into her mind. His sculpted abs that tapered into a trim waist and firm buttocks. The Keltic tattoo that took up most of his left arm and scrawled onto his chest. Those dark eyes that varied between brown and black, and never missed a damn thing. His shaggy black hair that hung boyishly over his forehead.

It had been almost ten years since she had seen him. The last time she set eyes on the man she was covered in blood after rescuing him from the evil Red Queen.

Alice had thought he would come and thank her, but he never had. For weeks and months, she glanced up, anticipation written on her face, hoping that it was the dark-eyed devil walking through her door.

But he hadn't come.

Weeks turned into months, and then years, and the sisters had found their place in Wonderland.

"No."

Harry's eyes bulged, "What do you mean, no?"

"Hell no," Alice said firmly, ire starting to lick her veins. "How dare that bastard make demands of me? I saved his ass, and this is how he thinks to repay me, by throwing me to the wolves?"

"He wanted to work together, Alice," Harry tried to soothe her, "Like a partnership."

Her dark eyes blazed, "He can shove his partnership up his ass, and if you come around here again asking favors of that man, you will find something shoved up yours as well."

Harry squeaked and raced out of the café, not even waiting to hear the little bells tinkle as the door opened which everyone knew was his favorite.

He rubbed his fluffy red hair worriedly. Jay wouldn't be happy to hear that Alice refused him. He wasn't the same kid they once knew.

He topped six foot five and was a solid wall of muscle, that was in his human form. Harry shuddered to think about when Jay took the Jabberwocky form.

Maybe, he could trick them into a meeting. That way Alice couldn't blame him, and Jay would get what he wanted?

Smiling, Harry scampered off to work on his new plan, unaware that Lory had been watching him the entire time from the back door with a knowing look on her face.

Finish reading in: Jabberwocky (Wicked Wonderland: Down the Rabbit Hole)

ABOUT THE AUTHOR

About the Author

USA TODAY Bestselling Author S. CINDERS is a multi-genre award-winning author of romance. She loves writing everything from contemporary billionaire romances to swashbuckling pirate tales or writing of alpha shifters to deadly vampires to fractured fairy tales to alien abductions.

S. CINDERS lives in the Midwest with her husband and two teenage sons who keep her on her toes. Known as the naughty romance author, you will remember her for her banter and engaging characters. Once you start, you won't want to stop!

Get insider information on new releases, FREE story, and more by joining S. CINDERS newsletter.

Neverpeak Mountain
Magestic Mountain
Mermaid Lagoon
Pirate Island
Maze of Regret
Tiki Forest
Neverland
Neverbay

Skull Rock
Cannibal Cove
Lost Boys Hideout
Pixie Hollow
Crocodile Creek
Pirate's Cove
Indian Tribe

Made in United States
Cleveland, OH
21 January 2025

13663912R00144